**They swayed bac**  **the night breezes in the way she wi upon a time, he h way; always chaste, yet always as sweet and sensual as a touch could ever be. She kept her eyes straight ahead, which meant looking at his collarbone. That was far better than looking into his eyes again, because she knew that if she did, she would come undone.**

As the vocalist hit a particularly high note, Chris placed his bent index finger beneath her chin. Wordlessly, he tilted her face upward, effectively forcing her to look at him. He said nothing, letting the intensity of his gaze speak for him.

Eliza gasped, but couldn't look away. She remembered a time when he'd had full possession of her heart, and when she looked into his coal dark eyes, it was as if that time had never ended.

In that moment, it became clear why all her relationships had failed. Her feelings for Chris lingered on, despite their long separation. She wondered if she could ever really be free of the power he held over her, the power of first love.

Hi there!

I hope you'll enjoy *A San Diego Romance*, my contribution to the Millionaire Moguls series. I was uncertain how this would all turn out since I've never done a group project quite like this before, but I think it turned out well. And I couldn't be more thrilled to be working with Yahrah St. John and Reese Ryan. Check out Chris and Eliza's love story, and let me know your thoughts on Facebook (Facebook.com/kiannawrites), Twitter (@kiannawrites) or Instagram (@kiannaalexanderwrites).

All the best,

*Kianna*

# *A* SAN DIEGO *Romance*

Kianna Alexander

HARLEQUIN® KIMANI™ ROMANCE

Special thanks and acknowledgment are given to
Kianna Alexander for her contribution to
the Millionaire Moguls miniseries.

Recycling programs
for this product may
not exist in your area.

ISBN-13: 978-1-335-21667-0

A San Diego Romance

**H HARLEQUIN®**

™ www.Harlequin.com

**Printed in U.S.A.**

**Kianna Alexander**, like any good Southern belle, wears many hats: loving wife, doting mama, advice-dispensing sister and gabbing girlfriend. She's a voracious reader, an amateur seamstress and occasional painter in oils. Chocolate, American history, sweet tea and Idris Elba are a few of her favorite things. A native of the Tar Heel state, Kianna still lives there with her husband, two kids and a collection of well-loved vintage '80s Barbie dolls. You can keep up with Kianna's releases and appearances by signing up for her mailing list at: www.authorkiannaalexander.com/sign-up.

### Books by Kianna Alexander

### Harlequin Kimani Romance

For all those who love a sailor, soldier,
airman, marine or other servicemember.
Thank you for lending your loved ones to our nation.

# Chapter 1

Coffee mug in hand, Christopher Marland took a seat on one end of the black leather sofa inside the San Diego office of Prescott George. It was quiet for a Wednesday morning, or maybe it just seemed that way to him. As an architect who'd created designs for buildings all over the world, and a divorced parent of teenage twins, he had a million things on his mind. One of his most important roles, though, was here, as the president of the San Diego chapter of Prescott George, a club of sorts for African American millionaires. And at the moment, the problems plaguing the organization were foremost in his mind.

Vaughn Ellicott, an old friend who served as treasurer of Prescott George, sat on the opposite end of the sofa, drinking from his own mug. "Listen, Chris. We need to talk about what happened at Jordan's studio."

Chris felt his face crease into a frown at the mention of the incident. Jordan Jace, a gifted sculptor and fellow member of Prescott George, had recently had one of his sculptures vandalized during a Prescott George party he'd hosted at his gallery. That would be upsetting enough in itself, but there was more to it. "I'm still pissed that he would accuse Jojo." Chris wasn't the type of parent to believe his children could do no wrong, but he knew his daughter. "Jojo isn't a troublemaker."

"You don't have to tell me. I know Jojo's a good kid."

"I mean, I drop thousands every year for her and Jack to go to one of the best private schools in the city." Chris ran his free hand over his head. "She makes the honor roll every nine weeks, she does her chores and she never gives me a bit of trouble."

"Jordan was bugging, Chris. It was probably just the stress of the whole incident that had him talking crazy like that." Vaughn took another long draw from the mug. "Try to cut him some slack."

While he understood that Jordan had been upset, Chris still didn't like the way things had gone down. He felt insulted on his daughter's behalf. "I know, I know. But I'm just not sure what to do here. I can't go for him talking about my daughter that way. And at this point, he's just piling on. There's already so much bad press out there about us right now."

Vaughn nodded. "Right. With the break-in here, and now this vandalism thing, we're looking way more scandalous than I would prefer."

"You and me both. As chapter president, all this drama reflects badly on me." Chris sighed, drinking down about half his coffee in one long swig. The way this day was going, he would need the caffeine. "And the timing of all this couldn't be worse. We finally got the Chapter of the Year nod, we've got a gala coming up in less than six weeks and everything seems to be going to the left."

With a rueful shake of his head, Vaughn asked, "So, what are we going to do about all this?"

"We've got to think strategically, then find the underlying cause of this mess before the chapter goes down in flames."

"Right. Can you think of anybody who might

be holding a grudge against us? Either as a chapter, or as an organization as a whole?"

Chris shrugged. "Not off the top of my head."

Vaughn set his mug aside. "I know it's a sensitive subject, man, but I have to ask. Do you think Sheila might have been involved in any of this?"

Feeling his frown deepen at the mention of her name, Chris admitted, "It's possible. I certainly wouldn't put it past her." His ex-wife was about as vindictive and petty as a person could be. Even though they saw as little of each other as possible these days, Chris couldn't cut her out of his life because of their twins, Jack and Jojo. "I know for a fact she enjoys seeing me miserable."

"She's a real piece of work, your ex." Vaughn's phone vibrated, and he looked at the screen briefly before pocketing it.

"You're telling me. I never should have married her." When Chris had met Sheila, he'd been on the heels of a serious heartbreak. She'd slid right in to comfort him, and a few months later, she'd announced her pregnancy. "I mean, I don't regret my kids. They were really the only good thing to come out of our relationship."

Vaughn smiled. "They're amazing kids, Chris."

"Thanks." Inwardly, he agreed. Jack and Jojo were the best part of his life. He simply wished he could say the same about the circumstances that brought them into this world. He sighed then, wondering if his dealings with women would ever come without the drama. "I don't know, man. Maybe I'm just not meant to be coupled up. Seems to me my life goes a lot smoother when I'm on my own."

"That's what you think now. But if the right one ever comes along, you'll change your mind." Vaughn's grin broadened.

"You and Miranda are different." Chris knew Vaughn was talking about his new wife, and he was happy for his friend. What Vaughn didn't know was that the "right one" had already come and gone. Chris had probably already blown his shot at true happiness.

"If you say so. Hey, what's going on with that latest design project you were after?"

Chris felt his mood lighten as Vaughn changed the subject. "Oh, you mean the new Museum of Sustainable Art? I won the bid."

Vaughn moved closer, gave Chris a slap on the back. "You snagged it? Hey, congratulations, man."

"Thanks, V."

"So, what's this museum going to be all about?"

Chris scratched his chin as he recalled the description given to him by the developer. "They plan to showcase modern art and sculpture that was created using only green supplies, tools and methods. Should be a pretty interesting place once it's open."

"Sounds like it." Vaughn stood then and grabbed his mug. "You done? I'm taking mine to the sink."

Chris handed off his mug and watched as Vaughn strode off, disappearing into the small kitchen to deposit the two cups.

When Vaughn returned, he asked, "When are the final blueprints due for this one?"

"I've got a couple of months. They want to break ground in September."

"I see. Well, I'm sure you'll live up to your world renown and blow them away with your design." The loud buzzing of Vaughn's phone sounded then. He checked the screen, then said, "Excuse me, man. I've gotta take this."

Chris nodded, settling back into his seat while Vaughn stepped around the corner to answer the call. He let his mind wander then, away from the stress of his daily life and back to the beautiful face of the only woman who'd ever really had his heart. He could still picture her clearly, despite the years that had passed since he'd last seen her.

He felt the smile tilt his lips at the memory of her soft bronze skin, full lips and expressive brown eyes. She'd brought so much joy into his life, yet somehow, he'd been fool enough to let his fears come between them. He'd walked away from her, driven away by the threats of what would happen to his career if he stayed. To this day, he still regretted that decision.

Vaughn returned then, his face creased with worry. "Something's going down at Elite, Chris. I gotta go." Vaughn owned an exclusive surf wear company, and he was as passionate about his business as he was about surfing.

Chris balked. "Is it serious? Does it involve PG?"

"I don't know. Maybe."

"What about lunch?"

Vaughn shrugged as he headed for the door. "I'm not sure, but I hope I'll be back by then. I'll let you know." On the heels of his words, he left.

Alone in the office, Chris wondered what was going on at Elite.

He also wondered what Vaughn would think had he known Chris was fantasizing about Vaughn's baby sister.

As Eliza Ellicott walked through the glass door, entering the Prescott George office, she glanced around the familiar surroundings. The interior was quiet, and she wondered again what exactly the guys did here. *Where's Vaughn?* Knowing her older brother, he'd probably gotten caught up in something and forgotten their plans for the day.

She went down the hall, encountering no one. She knew that since the door was open, somebody had to be there. When she stepped into the main lobby area, her gaze landed on the black leather sofa.

She jumped when she saw Christopher Marland reclining there, reading a newspaper. He wore a dark suit, crisp white shirt and emerald green tie.

He looked up, a smile crossing his handsome face when he saw her. "Eliza. It's been ages. How are you?"

Seeing him had her so out of sorts, all she could manage was to squeak out a hello.

His smile broadened. "Come on in. What brings you to Prescott George?"

She couldn't help staring at his dark gorgeousness. The smile highlighted his full lips and chiseled jawline and put a sparkle in his coffee-hued eyes. Realizing she couldn't continue to stand there like a deer in the high beams, she shook herself free of his spell as best she could. "I…

uh… Where's Vaughn? I was supposed to meet him for lunch."

His expression changed. "Oh, sorry. You just missed him."

She sighed. "Crap."

"He got a call from Elite and rushed over there." He folded the newspaper and set it aside. "I'm guessing there was some emergency that needed his attention."

Her stomach rumbled. She'd been at the counter at her boutique, Ellicott's, for four solid hours, and now her body demanded sustenance. "I guess that means I'm on my own for lunch, then." She turned, intent on leaving the same way she'd come.

"Wait." Chris's deep voice gave her pause.

She turned back his way. "What is it?"

"Listen, why don't you stay and have lunch with me? I mean, you already drove all the way over here." He stood then, his height towering over her.

She pulled her fallen purse strap back up on her shoulder and swallowed. Christopher Marland, the man who'd broken her heart fourteen years ago, was inviting her to have lunch with him. Alone. She doubted he even knew how crushed she'd been by his leaving. Logic told her to get the hell out of there as fast as her black pumps would carry her. "I don't know, Chris."

He moved closer then, entering her personal bubble. "I ordered from the Lotus Flower, that new Asian fusion sushi place. At the time, I thought Vaughn would be here, so I ordered enough for two."

"I, well…" She looked away from his penetrating gaze, feeling herself taken in by his charm. He had a way about him, something that seemed to melt her resistance. His scent, clean and masculine, threatened to overwhelm her. Her inner voice reminded her of good sense, while her stomach reminded her of how much she loved sushi.

"I know you're probably really busy, so you don't have to stay long. But I'd hate for the food to go to waste."

Her stomach growled again, louder this time. She looked his way, hoping he hadn't heard it.

His grin told her he had.

Hunger won out over logic, in more ways than one. She drew a deep breath. "I'll stay."

"Great. Food should be here soon." He gestured to the circular table and four chairs occupying a corner of the room. "Care to sit down?"

She watched him slide out a chair and stand behind it. When she sat down, he pushed her chair up to the table before taking the seat across from her.

"Still a gentleman, I see." The remark slipped out before she could stop it.

"Always." He fixed her with a knowing gaze.

The sound of the glass door opening stopped any further chatter. He stood. "Must be the delivery guy. I'll get it."

She sat alone, trying to get her mind right. A few moments later, he returned with the plastic bag. The scent of the food made her stomach grumble again, but she was grateful to have something to distract her from Chris's distinctive aroma.

As he set the large paper bag of food on the table, she pulled out her travel-sized hand sanitizer. After doing her hands, she offered it to him.

"Thanks." He used it, then passed the bottle back to her and started setting the food out.

At first, they ate in silence, and she devoured three California rolls. Swallowing a bite, she looked up and saw his gaze resting on her face. "Um, sorry. I was pretty hungry."

He shrugged. "No biggie. Tell me, how are things at Ellicott's?"

That brought a smile to her face. "Great. I've recently started to carry some clothes and accessories by a new designer. Her name is Bea Phillips, and her items are selling as soon as I can get them in."

Taking a swig from his bottled water, he asked, "So, what kinds of things does she design?"

"Mainly dresses, but she also makes jewelry and handbags." She forked up some of her jasmine rice.

"I'm glad to hear business is booming. Back in the day, you would always talk about owning your own boutique." He tucked his empty plastic tray back into the paper bag. "I knew you'd do it one day."

"I'm surprised you remember the things we talked about back then," she said absently. "In a lot of ways, that all seems like ancient history." Or at least that's what she told herself. She'd been heartbroken when they parted ways, but he didn't know that, and she intended to keep it that way. Besides, she'd done well for herself, both personally and professionally. She'd managed to get the store established and off the ground. And rather than close herself off to romantic relationships, she'd had a string of steady boyfriends, all from prominent social circles. No one could say she'd gone into hiding after Chris left.

"You'd be surprised by all the things I remember." He smiled as he tipped the water bottle and drained the remaining contents.

Hearing what he'd said, and thinking of the implications of that, made her quickly change the subject. "I don't know if Vaughn talks about our sisters much, but they're both married with kids now."

He nodded. "I know. Vaughn talks about Brianne and Emily on occasion. I know he loves being an uncle."

She thought back to the conversations they'd had years ago about her dreams. What he didn't know was how she'd dreamed of being a mother and wife in addition to running her store. Back then, she'd thought she could have it all. Reality had shown her something different. "I'm the only girl in the family to strike out on her own to conquer the business world."

"Nothing wrong with that, especially when you're successful at what you do." He gestured to her near-empty tray. "Are you done?"

She nodded, tucking her trash into the paper bag.

He left the table to throw all the garbage away, then returned to his seat across from her. Stretching, he said, "Yeah. Growing up an only child made me want a big family of my own. Things didn't exactly go as planned, but I have Jack and Jojo now, and I couldn't be more grateful for them."

She felt her heart constrict in her chest at his words. His marriage to his ex-wife had come right on the heels of their breakup, effectively dashing her hopes of reconciliation between them. And now, despite the utter failure of the marriage, he'd still gotten one thing she wanted just as much as she wanted success in business: children. Still, she hid her feelings behind a practiced smile. "How are the kids? They're teenagers now, aren't they? I hear that's an adventure."

"Yeah, they're thirteen now. They're a handful, for sure. I get them every other weekend."

"What are kids really like at this age?"

"They're still kids, but they think of themselves as adults, so that's hard to navigate." He straightened in his chair. "There are times when I feel torn between work and doing things with them, and sometimes they have their own plans and don't want to be stuck with me." He shrugged. "I just do my best, take it one day at a time. They know I love them, and that's the most important thing."

She nodded, keeping the smile plastered on her face. Inside, she mused that if she and Chris had gotten married, their children would be about Jack and Jojo's age. She didn't dare open her mouth, lest her thoughts become words.

He smiled again then. "I'm really glad you came by, Eliza. It's so good to see you again."

She averted her eyes from his arresting handsomeness, only made more appealing by his expression. Was he flirting with her? Her feminine instincts told her he was. Why would he do that now, after all these years apart?

The man he used to be was long gone, as was the young, idealistic girl she'd once been. What she saw before her now was a divorced workaholic who'd walked away from her when he had the chance to make things official.

As far as she was concerned, there was nothing left for her and Chris.

# Chapter 2

Chris was enjoying spending time with Eliza. It had been ages since he'd seen her, and having her grace him with her beautiful presence again lit the dark corners of his heart. She seemed a little guarded, and he supposed he understood that, after the abrupt ending of their relationship. Still, he couldn't deny the feelings this woman elicited in him. He'd thought of her often over the years, and had always known he was still attracted to her. Being in the same room with her now showed him just how strong his feelings still were.

*She's even more beautiful than I remember.*

While they spoke, he looked over her glossy dark hair, her pink lipstick and the dark fringe of lashes framing her sparkling eyes. Even the way she sat across from him, with one long, bare leg crossed demurely over the other, enthralled him.

"I mean, they're teenagers," he continued. "Sometimes I don't understand a word they're saying. But at least I'm never bored."

She stood then, her movement abrupt. "I think I've stayed too long." As she spoke, she smoothed her palms over the formfitting sheath she wore, as if brushing away imaginary wrinkles.

Chris stood, too, caught off guard by her action. Moments ago, they'd been chatting about his twins, and she'd been smiling and nodding. Now, her closed-off expression and tense stance gave him pause. "You don't have to rush off, Eliza. There's not too much going on here today."

She slipped her purse strap over her shoulder. "It's just that I really have to get back to the boutique. I've got a million things to do this afternoon."

He wanted to convince her to stay, but how could he? She wasn't the starry-eyed teenager who'd stolen his heart anymore; she was a successful businesswoman with responsibilities. Even though the woman she'd become appealed to him in every way, he knew he had no right to hold her there. "I understand. I won't keep you, if you've got…" His sentence was cut off by the ringing of his cell phone. He slipped it from his pocket, glanced at it. "I have to take this. Excuse me, Eliza."

"I've got to go, Chris." She started walking toward the hallway.

"Just give me a few moments, please. I want to at least see you out, okay?"

She stopped, turned his way. "All right."

He answered his phone then. "Jojo? How are you, sweetheart?"

"I'm okay, I guess."

Sensing the angst in her words, he asked, "What do you need, Jojo?"

"Well, there's this dance coming up at school. Mom says I can go, if you say it's okay. So, can I go?"

The parts of him that still saw her as a little girl warred with the reality of her actual age. Finally, he acquiesced. "Sure. Who are you going with?" Relief coursed through him as she named two of her female friends.

"There's one more thing. I really need a dress."

"A dress?" Chris looked at Eliza. She was leaning against the wall between the kitchen and the hallway. "Jojo, I may be able to help you with that." Covering the microphone, he gestured to her. "Eliza, can you come here for a second?"

She walked over, a curious expression on her face. "What is it?"

"I know you have to go, but my daughter's on the phone. She needs a dress for a school dance. Can you help us out?"

"Maybe. What size does she wear?"

He scratched his head. "I don't know. I could ask her…"

Eliza's lips tilted in a soft smile. "She's thirteen, right? I remember those days well. Why don't you just bring her to the shop Friday?" She glanced at her gold watch. "I really do have to go."

"What time should I bring her?" he asked as Eliza strode away.

"Around six," she answered as she rounded the corner to the hallway.

A few moments later, Chris heard the door to the office open, then close as she walked out. Uncovering the mic, he spoke to his daughter. "Good news. Friday, I'll take you shopping for a dress."

Jojo exhaled. "Thanks, Dad." Then she paused. "Wait. You're not going to take me to the little girl's section of Macy's again, are you?"

He chuckled at the memory of how their last

shopping trip had panned out. "No, no. I'm taking you to a boutique in Gaslamp. Don't worry, you'll love it."

"Sounds great. When?"

"I'll pick you up around five Friday evening. We'll grab dinner and head over after that."

Her voice took on the light, happy tone of a girl pleased with her father. "You're the best, Dad. Gotta go. Love you."

He smiled, both at her words and at knowing she was excited. "I love you, too."

After he disconnected the call, he looked around the quiet office. He and Vaughn had been the only members in the building today, and now that Eliza had gone, he was alone save for the security guard patrolling the place. In truth, he needed this time alone to think. The problems at Prescott George were pressing, and he needed the space and silence to determine the best course of action. As chapter president, the responsibility rested on his shoulders.

Chris knew full well what an honor it was for it to be chosen for the Chapter of the Year award. The San Diego chapter members were a younger set compared with the old guard of the original members' descendants in some of the other chapters. Prescott George had been around for a long time, and not everyone embraced the necessary changes that came with changing times. Still, if the national organization had seen fit to recognize his chapter, then Chris would make damn sure that San Diego PG lived up to those lofty expectations.

Now, though, he had something else on his mind; an almost welcome distraction. He'd been shocked and amazed to see Eliza Ellicott stroll into the office, looking every bit like his dream come true. Here he was, at the top of his game in the architecture field, with his designs having been used for structures all around the world. Yet when she'd walked in, he'd felt…outdone, as if she were way out of his league. He could have spent all day talking to her, watching her smile light the room. While he didn't like that she'd been inconvenienced by her brother, he was glad fate had decided to let him enjoy her company again.

He thought of Vaughn then and wondered what was going on at Elite. Lunch had long since ended, and Vaughn hadn't reached out yet. Chris pulled out his phone again, intent on calling his friend before he continued strategizing his plans for the chapter.

After all, if it was something serious, he needed to know so he could lend a hand. He could only hope whatever was going down at Elite wasn't tied to Prescott George. Their chapter had enough problems already.

Ellicott's did brisk business on the weekends, and Friday evening was no exception. Eliza and her two clerks were all working, with Eliza bagging purchases and the clerks running the registers.

As Eliza passed one of her signature glossy silver paper bags filled with items to a customer, she heard the bell ring, signaling someone entering the shop. After the customer was taken care of, she glanced toward the door and saw Chris walking in her direction.

Eliza couldn't help admiring him as he walked. Dressed in a dark blue polo shirt, matching sneakers and a pair of khaki shorts that revealed his muscled calves, he looked ready to head down to the marina for a day on the bay.

At his side was a pretty young lady in ripped white jeans, a *Candy Crush* T-shirt and sneakers. She was tall for her age; the top of her head lined up with Chris's shoulder. Her dark brown hair, styled in box braids, hung just past her collarbone. Much of her face was concealed by the round frames of a very large pair of white-rimmed sunglasses.

The pair walked up to the counter, and Chris smiled as he made eye contact with her. "Hi, Eliza. Thanks for doing this for me."

She swallowed a lump in her throat. The combination of his smile and his tone made her awareness of him rise. "No problem." She reached across the counter and stuck out her hand to the young lady. "You must be Jojo. I'm Eliza, nice to meet you."

"Yes. Hi." Jojo removed her sunglasses.

Eliza's breath caught when she saw Chris's eyes looking back at her. To say Jojo resembled Chris would be an understatement. "Wow. You look an awful lot like your father."

Jojo grinned. "Thanks, I think." Shaking hands with Eliza, she asked, "Dad told me to call you Ms. Ellicott. Can I call you by your first name?"

Eliza chuckled. "I'm fine with you using my first name, but I'll defer to your father."

Chris shrugged. "I don't mind if you don't."

"You can call me Eliza, then." She walked around the counter and stood between Chris and Jojo. "So, what kind of dress do you have in mind, Jojo?"

Jojo's expression showed her uncertainty. "I'm not really sure. It's my first real dance."

Eliza gave Chris a playful jab with her elbow. "You ready for this, Dad?"

Half smiling, he shook his head. "Don't ask. Let's just say I'm going along with it."

"Well, Jojo, if you trust me, I've got some ideas." She stood back, getting another look at her client. "With your height and figure, you'll have a lot of options.

She blushed. "Really?"

Eliza nodded. "Definitely. As a matter of fact, I've got some new dresses that just came in from a local designer that I think would be perfect for you."

Jojo's eyes widened. "New designer dresses?"

"Yep." Eliza reached out and linked arms with Jojo. "Come with me. I'll show you." She led her over to the right side of the store, where new merchandise was on display. "We can narrow it down if you tell me your favorite color."

Chris followed them, observing quietly.

Jojo, her eyes still wide, perused the racks of dresses in front of her. "I really like orange. Do you have anything in that color?"

Eliza tapped her chin for a moment, mentally going through the latest shipment. Then she snapped her fingers. "Yes." She moved over two racks from where Jojo and Chris stood and searched through the drawers holding merchandise she didn't have room to display on the racks or mannequins. When she found the dress she was looking for, she unfolded it and held it up. "What do you think?"

Jojo gasped. "OMG. It's gorgeous."

"When you said you liked orange, I thought you'd like this one." Eliza admired the sleeveless, calf-length dress. The V-neck line was subtle and adorned with crystals, as was the flounce at the hem. "It's so new it hasn't even been on display yet."

"Wow." Jojo took the dress from Eliza. Looking to Chris, she asked, "Can I try it on, Dad?"

"Sure." Chris smiled at his daughter. "Is this the only one you want to try on?"

Jojo looked back at Eliza. "Can I look through the racks?"

"Go ahead." Eliza watched as Jojo searched through the displays.

Jojo came back with two dresses. One was a soft shade of yellow and very low-cut in the front. The other, a coral minidress, couldn't possibly hit longer than midthigh on someone her height.

Chris began shaking his head almost immediately. "No way, young lady."

Jojo frowned. "Geez, Dad." She turned to Eliza, hoping for a reprieve. "What do you think?"

Eliza tapped her chin with her forefinger. She agreed with Chris: these two dresses were far too revealing for someone Jojo's age. Seeking to steer her in a better direction, she said, "I can see why you like them, but let's try these instead."

Her frown softening a bit, Jojo asked, "You have more dresses in mind for me?"

"Just a couple." Eliza put back the dresses Jojo had chosen and noted the relief on Chris's face. Then she moved through the store, pulling the other two dresses she thought might suit Jojo's age and tastes, and handed them over. "Come on, I'll set you up in a room."

Once Jojo was inside one of the five dressing rooms on the back wall of the store, Eliza leaned against the edge of the counter, awaiting the fashion show to come.

Chris, standing next to her, said, "You've got a gift. I can see you're very good at what you do here."

"I appreciate that." Eliza smiled his way. His compliment flattered her, probably more than it should have. Of course, it had always been that way. He'd been skilled at sweet-talking her back in the day, and he hadn't lost his touch.

"I'm amazed at how fast you built a rapport with California's most fickle teenage girl. Beyond that, you only chose dresses for her that were age appropriate, and she actually seemed to like them." Chris shook his head, his expression conveying his amazement. "When I try to pick out things for her, I just get the pouty face."

Eliza laughed. "Like I said, I remember what it was like to be her age. It's an awkward time, when all a girl wants is to be cool and fit in." It wasn't until Eliza was in her midtwenties that she truly understood the value of individualism, and embraced it.

Chris walked closer to her, entering her personal bubble the same way he had at Prescott George. "Well, you have my undying respect and gratitude."

"Still a smooth talker, I see." She turned toward him, her back against the edge of the counter.

"It's the truth." He took a step closer to her. "These aren't empty words to gas you up. I really feel that way."

Their gazes met and held, and Eliza found herself unable to turn away. How could he still have such a hold on her, after all this time? It seemed she'd done the right thing by avoiding him over the last several years.

They stood there that way, searching each other's eyes, for several long moments.

Jojo's voice broke into Eliza's thoughts.

"How do I look?"

Eliza, grateful for the distraction, drew a breath.

"We'll talk more later." Chris said the words for her ears only.

# Chapter 3

Chris's eyes lingered on Eliza's face a moment longer, then he directed his attention to his daughter.

Chris swung his gaze toward Jojo, who'd emerged from the dressing room in a soft orange A-line dress with a taffeta skirt.

"It's gorgeous." Eliza smiled in her direction. "Turn around so we can see it all."

The dress Jojo wore now wasn't the first one Eliza had handed her, but she did look beautiful in it. "I love it, sweetie. Very nice."

Eliza chimed in again. "What do you think of it, Jojo?"

Regarding her reflection in the mirrors in the corner, Jojo shrugged. "It's really pretty, but I don't know if it's the one I want."

Walking over to her, Eliza patted her on the shoulder. "That's fine. Go try on the others, then you can make your choice."

Jojo nodded, then disappeared back into the dressing room.

Anticipating this might take a while, Chris sat down on one of the three upholstered ottomans near the dressing room doors. He let his gaze sweep over the interior of Eliza's boutique. From the front door, he'd seen a lot of it, but from his current vantage point, he could see it all. The soft gray walls and carpet seemed to disappear behind her colorful assortment of clothing, jewelry and accessories. The layout of the store left plenty of space for customers to walk between the mannequins, racks and displays, and there was even a small conversation area with a sofa, two chairs and a coffee table, situated on the opposite side of the counter from the dressing rooms. Though he didn't know much about women's fashion, he could appreciate the work Eliza must have put into the design and setup of her store. She'd taken a space that, from an architectural perspective, was pretty basic, and transformed it into something welcoming and aesthetically pleasing.

He saw her talking to one of her staff members, and he could feel the smile tilting his lips. She probably thought the long, silent moment they'd spent before Jojo had come out to model the dress could be forgotten or tossed aside. He knew better. Though no words had been exchanged, the unspoken desire flowing between them had been obvious. He wouldn't press her about it now, because he'd come here for his daughter. Eventually, though, they were going to discuss what was happening between them.

Jojo came out then in the bedazzled orange dress Eliza had first chosen for her. Chris couldn't help smiling when he saw his daughter in the dress. It was tasteful, pretty and perfectly suited to her.

Grinning, Jojo came to stand by the mirrors. "Wow. This is it."

"I agree." Chris watched her do a slow turn, amazed at how grown-up his little girl suddenly looked.

Eliza came over then and began applauding as soon as she saw Jojo. "Oh, honey. You should get this one. It's perfect on you."

Jojo's eyes sparkled as she looked at her reflection from various angles. "Okay, Dad. This is the one I want."

"Great. Let's box it up." Chris stood. He loved spending time with his daughter, and with Eliza, but he didn't really want to spend his entire Friday night hanging out in a ladies' clothing store.

"Wait." Jojo walked away from the mirrors and grabbed Eliza's arms. "Now I need accessories. Can you help me find shoes, jewelry and maybe a bag?"

"Sure thing." Eliza glanced at Chris. "Give us a few minutes more, okay?"

Sitting back down, Chris nodded. "I'll be here."

He watched the pair search through the accessories displays on the front left side of the store and the shoe section next to them. He could hear some of their conversation about what was currently "in" right now, and their chatter about shoes, necklaces and handbags threatened to put him to sleep. Still, he could see the rapport growing between Eliza and Jojo, and from where he sat, his daughter even seemed impressed with his former sweetheart. Moody and unpredictable as Jojo could be, impressing her was no small feat.

When Jojo finally piled her things up on the counter for Eliza to ring up, Chris marveled at the size of the pile. "Do you really need all of this, Jojo?"

"Well, Dad, I got the dress for the dance, plus an extra one, just in case." Jojo picked up the items one by one as she explained. "Then I needed shoes, earrings, a necklace, a bracelet, this cute little bag…"

Chris put his hand up. "Okay, okay." He reached for his wallet as a smiling Eliza started tallying the bill.

Ten minutes and a few hundred dollars later, Eliza handed a metallic silver bag over the counter to Jojo. "Here you go, honey. Have fun at the dance."

Chris turned to leave, but Jojo hesitated.

"Can I have a minute, Dad?"

"Sure. I'll wait by the door." He walked away, taking up a post by the exit. From where he stood, he could hear them talking.

"I'd really like to be able to call you, if you don't mind." Jojo leaned over the counter. "That way I can find out when new stuff comes in, and get tips from you on fashion and stuff."

"I don't mind at all." A smiling Eliza took one of the store's business cards off the stack by the register and jotted something on the back. Passing it to Jojo, she winked. "Here's my number."

"Thanks. See you later." Jojo tucked the card into her hip pocket and walked toward where Chris stood waiting at the door.

As they stepped out into the cool evening air, Chris commented, "You really like Eliza, huh?"

"She seems cool." Jojo's tone was nonchalant. She waited for Chris to open the passenger-side door of his midsize sedan, then climbed in.

He shut his daughter in, then climbed into the driver's seat. While buckling up he asked, "Are you actually going to call her?"

Jojo chuckled. "I am. I wanna get the new stuff before everybody else does." She squirmed a bit and reached into her pocket. Handing him the card, she said, "So, be sure to return this to me after you call her."

Chris felt his eyes widen. "What?"

Jojo shook her head. "Come on, Dad. You're crushing on her. Anybody can see that."

"You're very perceptive."

"I know. That's why I knew you'd need my help."

Chris shook his head. Starting his car, he marveled at his daughter. "You're amazing. Thanks, Jojo."

"No problem, Dad. You can pay me back in new clothes."

A laughing Chris backed out of the parking spot and pulled out into the road.

Later that night, Chris pulled the Ellicott's business card out and punched the number into his phone.

"Hello?" Eliza's voice filled his ear as she answered the call.

"Hi, Eliza. It's me, Chris."

"Chris?" The surprise in her voice was soon replaced with acceptance. "Got my number from Jojo, right?"

He chuckled. "Yeah, she helped me out."

Eliza cleared her throat. "What can I do for you, Chris?"

He had many answers for that question, but he went with the most appropriate one. "I'm just calling to thank you for helping me out with Jojo today."

"It's no problem. She's a sweet kid, and I was happy to help."

"She's pretty hard to please these days, but bringing her to Ellicott's got me some major brownie points with her. I really appreciate it."

Eliza laughed, the sound soft and musical. "Like I said, no problem. Actually, you already thanked me, by spending all that money in my store. I'd say we're even."

"Still, I'd like to do something for you. Why don't you let me take you to dinner tomorrow night?"

She hesitated for a long moment. "I don't know, Chris."

"It's just dinner. You gotta eat, right?"

She exhaled in his ear, then gave in. "Okay, Chris. I'll go out with you, but it can't be any-place too fancy."

"We'll keep it casual, I promise." Chris grinned at the thought of spending time alone with Eliza after all these years. "What time should I pick you up?"

"Eight. You'll have to pick me up at the bou-tique."

"That's fine." He didn't know if she would be getting off work around that time, or she just didn't want him at her house, but it didn't really matter. "See you then. Good night, Eliza."

"Night, Chris." She disconnected the call.

Tucking his phone away, a smiling Chris strolled to the bathroom for a hot shower.

Saturday night, Eliza stepped out of Ellicott's at five minutes to eight and found Chris's car idling at the curb. She waved, walked toward the car.

He jumped out and held open the passenger door for her. "Good evening."

She raked an appreciative gaze over his body, encased in dark denim jeans and a fitted black T-shirt. "Hi, Chris." She slipped into the car and buckled up as he shut the door.

"You look nice," he remarked as he settled in next to her and started the car.

She looked down at her tan slacks and white cap-sleeve blouse. "Thanks. It's just what I wore to work today. You did say it would be casual."

"It will be." He pulled away from the curb.

They stopped off for dinner at the Burger Lounge on Fifth Avenue. It wasn't far from Ellicott's, and Eliza loved the food there. She chowed down on the cage-free turkey burger, while Chris enjoyed the classic Lounge burger. They shared a mixed basket of fries and onion rings.

Conversation flowed easily between them, and Eliza almost felt like they'd never been apart. "So, tell me about some of the buildings you've designed. Are there any around here that I might know?"

"Sure. But there's so many of them, it would be easier to just drive you around the city and show them to you." He popped an onion ring into his mouth.

Her eyebrow lifted. "Oh, really?" Was that his way of asking her out again? They'd only been together for about an hour on this outing.

He nodded. "Yes, really. There are about fifteen buildings in different locations around San Diego that are original Marland designs." He wiped his mouth with a napkin. "But it's up to you whether you want the tour."

Finishing her meal, Eliza tossed a crumpled napkin into the empty basket that had held the fries and onion rings. "I'm stuffed. Now I just want to crawl into bed."

"You know it's bad for your digestion to lie down right after you eat." He stood, cleared away their trash and threw it away. When he returned, he held out his hand to help her up. "Lucky for you, our night isn't over yet."

She looked up at him, confused. "We're going somewhere else?"

"Yes. And I promise you'll love it."

She pursed her lips. "All right now, Chris. We had dinner, like you asked. How long are you planning to keep me up tonight?" Too late, she realized the implications of what she'd said.

A wicked smile crossed over his face. "Not much longer. Don't worry. I'll have you home by eleven."

Shaking her head, she let him lead her out of the restaurant and back to the car.

She watched the passing scenery as they drove through the darkened streets. It was around nine thirty, and the vibrant night life in San Diego meant there was still a decent amount of traffic. Everything she saw was familiar; she'd grown up here and had returned home to open the boutique about six months ago. Still, gazing out the window was the best way she could think of to suppress the urge to openly stare at Chris.

He'd always been handsome, but now he was even more so. He'd aged like fine wine, and his success in the architecture field only added to his attractiveness. In the confines of the car, there was nothing to dampen the clean, masculine scent of his cologne. He smelled fantastic, and if she recalled correctly, he wore the same scent now as he had back when they'd dated.

She hazarded a glance his way, but didn't dare look at his face. Instead, she looked at his hand on the gearshift as he drove. The powerful engine of the car responded to his every command, the sound changing in time with his movements. The vehicle was under his complete control, and Eliza knew that if they didn't stop soon so she could get some fresh air, she would be, too.

He pulled into the parking lot at the San Diego Zoo, and Eliza's brow furrowed in confusion. "What are you doing, Chris? The zoo closes at nine."

"I know it does. For everybody else." He winked as he cut the engine.

That only confused Eliza more, but when he came around to the passenger side to open her door, she took his hand. The only way to find out what he meant was to follow him, so she did.

An employee opened the locked gates for them and ushered them in. "Good evening, Mr. Marland, Ms. Ellicott."

"Hi." Eliza turned her questioning gaze to Chris. "What's going on?"

He tipped the employee, then started walking toward Front Street. "It turns out that if you make a generous donation to the zoo's improvement fund, you can have the place all to yourself for a private tour."

She blinked a few times. "You mean…"

"Yep. There aren't any other visitors here."

Amazed, she asked, "What are we supposed to do in an empty zoo?"

He chuckled. "It's not like the animals and their caregivers went home, you know."

She rolled her eyes. "You know what I mean."

He guided her down the footpath through Koalafornia Boardwalk. "I remembered how much you loved the koalas, so I thought we'd spend some time at the koala exhibit."

She felt the smile stretching her lips as they passed through the carnival-like section of the zoo that led to the koalas. "You remember that? That was ages ago."

They crossed through Bieler Plaza and into the Outback section where the koala exhibit was located. "Of course I do. Remember when we came here that summer after you came home from freshman year of college?"

She smiled at the memory. "I remember. I was at the height of my koala obsession." She found the animals adorable, and right now, she thought Chris was pretty cute, too. "You bought me that giant stuffed koala from the gift shop. I still have it...somewhere."

"You kept it all these years, huh?" He placed a hand over his heart. "I'm touched that you held on to it."

She couldn't help laughing at his silliness.

They approached the koala exhibit and were greeted by a uniformed employee who introduced herself with a smile. "I'm Alice, and I'll be facilitating your experience tonight."

After greetings were exchanged, they were led behind the exhibit to a small building. Eliza was delighted as she and Chris were treated to a private, up-close look at the twenty or so koalas in the habitat. She watched them nibble eucalyptus leaves, saw them napping in quiet corners of the yard, and even saw a few joeys huddled against their mothers. As they watched the scene, Alice regaled them with many interesting facts about the cute furry creatures.

By the time they left, Eliza felt gleeful. She'd never forget her experience tonight. Turning to Chris as they walked back to his car, she said genuinely, "Thank you for this. It was amazing."

"I did promise you'd enjoy it, didn't I?" He reached for her hand.

She let him hold her hand. After what he'd just done for her, he deserved that much. "I can't believe you'd do all this for me." The gesture had been incredibly sweet, and far beyond what any of her other boyfriends had ever done for her.

"Why not, Eliza? This is how you deserve to be treated."

She looked up into his eyes, saw the sincerity there. Dragging her gaze away before she fell under his spell, she faked a yawn. "What time is it?"

He looked at his wristwatch. "After ten."

"You can just drop me back at Ellicott's. My car is there."

Once they were both strapped into their seats, he did as she asked.

Back at the boutique, he walked her to her car. "I had a great time tonight, Eliza. And I'd really like to see you again."

Her breath caught when she heard his softly spoken words. Her heart pounded in her ears with all the intensity of a Max Roach drum solo. Parts of her were elated, but other parts of her were… unsure. "I don't know, Chris."

"I don't want to pressure you. But I had to let you know how I feel."

She exhaled slowly. "Tell you what. Let me think about it, and I'll get back to you."

He offered a slight smile. "Fair enough. Good night, Eliza."

"Good night, Chris."

After she pulled out, she looked in her rear-view mirror and saw him idling at the curb for a moment before he hung a U-turn and drove off into the night.

## Chapter 4

Chris spent the better part of Saturday night lying awake. In the center of a king-size bed, with an extra-firm mattress, seven-hundred-thread-count sheets and extra-plush pillows, he should have slept peacefully. He'd closed his eyes, shifted positions, willed himself to seek rest. Despite his efforts, thoughts of Eliza kept him up, in more ways than one.

As he lay alone in the darkness, visions of her beautiful face filled his mind. She'd always been lovely, but now she'd fully grown into her beauty. She was savvy, successful and doing what she loved. He knew well the joy of turning one's passion into a career, and her enjoyment showed through in the way she ran her boutique.

Then, on top of all her wonderful qualities, she'd been patient and helpful with Jojo. He couldn't remember the last time he'd seen his daughter get along so well with someone she'd just met. Jojo had used the word *cool* to describe Eliza, and that was very high praise coming from a teenage girl.

*She's perfect.* Or at least, as close to perfect as a man could ever hope for. Fate had brought her into the office a few days ago. Now he wanted her back in his life, for good. He could still see the conflicted expression she'd worn when he asked to see her again. It seemed like she wanted him to, but something was stopping her from giving him a chance. What was holding her back from him? What was she afraid of?

He had no answers to those questions, and before he could decide how to assuage her fears, exhaustion got the better of him.

Over the next few days, he stayed close to home. Most of his time was spent in the well-appointed office he'd included in the floor plan of his one-of-a-kind home. The house, a supermodern structure built of white marble and impact-resistant glass, sat nestled into a hillside high above the city. The property boasted an underground garage, an infinity pool and panoramic views of the city and the bay below. His office, located on the second floor, had one entire wall made of glass that overlooked the pool.

Chris spent hours at his drafting table, finetuning his design for the Museum of Sustainable Art. Based on the museum's mission statement, the building would be built with as many recycled building materials as structurally possible, while still maintaining an attractive and safe result. The parameters of the job presented a unique challenge, but Chris embraced it. This project gave him a rare opportunity to stretch his creative mind and take his art to a higher plane. He used his straightedge to map out lines and wrote notes in the margins of the drafting paper as he worked.

During the day, while he lost himself in the passionate pursuit of the perfect design for the museum, he could push away his thoughts of Eliza. At night, however, when he set down his pencils and left the office, she haunted him like a specter. He ordered in for dinner, watched television, read the sports and business news online. No matter what he did, if he wasn't working, he found himself thinking of her.

He wondered why she hadn't called him yet with a decision on whether she'd go out with him again. Part of him held out hope; after all, how long did it take to say no? He surmised she would have called sooner if she meant to turn him down.

Tuesday night, as he perused one of his favorite business blogs, he felt his cell phone vibrating on his hip. Checking the display, he answered the phone right away. "Hello?"

"Hi, Chris. It's Eliza."

He knew that, because he'd saved her number in his phone when he called her the first time. *So, she finally decided to call.* He wanted to ask her if she'd made a decision, but he held back. Remembering his promise not to pressure her, he kept his tone casual. "It's good to hear from you. What's up?"

"I wanted to talk to you about Jojo, and the things you bought from the boutique."

His eyebrow hitched. This was not what he'd expected to hear when she called him. "What's there to talk about? You were a great help, she loved the things we bought and I dropped a nice chunk of change in the store. We're all happy, right?"

"Well, I thought we were." Eliza paused for a moment. "But apparently that wasn't the case."

Confused, he set his laptop aside and asked, "What do you mean?"

"Everything's been returned."

His brow crinkled. "Now, wait a minute. I saw Jojo's face, and there's no way she would have…"

"She didn't, Chris. Sheila brought everything back."

Chris drew in a breath and cringed. "Oh, no."

"Oh, yes." Eliza cleared her throat. "Sheila seemed quite displeased with all the items. She basically told me that she'd pick out her own daughter's dresses, and that she didn't require my 'interference.'"

"Oh, no." Chris knew he'd repeated himself, but he couldn't think of anything else to say. Hearing that his ex-wife had gone into Ellicott's and acted that way mortified him. "I'm so sorry this happened, Eliza."

"It isn't your fault. Obviously, she wasn't satisfied with what Jojo brought home."

More like, she wasn't satisfied with who the items were purchased from. He imagined Jojo had gone home, chattering on about Eliza and how cool she was, and that just hearing Eliza's name had set Sheila off. "It's not your fault, either. Your products are great quality, and my daughter loved them. This is just Sheila's way. She can't resist an opportunity to stir up drama."

Eliza sighed. "Jojo did seem really happy with what she picked out. I wonder if she even knows her mother returned everything."

"Probably not. Again, I'm really sorry about all this."

"It's okay."

He took a deep breath. "I'm really glad you called, Eliza. It's nice to hear your voice again. To be honest, I was starting to think I wasn't going to hear from you."

She released a cute little chuckle. "The funny thing is, I probably wouldn't have called today if your ex hadn't shown up in the store."

"Hmm. In that case, Sheila did me a favor."

"Chris, I really don't want to cause problems between you and Sheila. Since she's the twins' mother, you two have to be able to be cordial, at least."

"Don't worry about it. Conflict is about all Sheila and I will ever have." He shifted on the sofa, turning to the side so he could prop his feet up. "Trust me, if it weren't you, she'd find some other reason to be upset with me."

"Maybe so, Chris, but I wouldn't feel right about making things more difficult between you two. I can understand why Sheila doesn't want another woman spending time with her daughter, and…"

"Eliza, I hate to interrupt you, but you seem overly concerned about my ex and her preferences." He paused. "What about you? What do *you* want?"

Eliza blinked a few times, caught off guard by Chris's question. "What?"

"I asked you what you want. Stop thinking about Sheila, because she's a nonfactor. Consider how *you* want to proceed." His emphasis on the word *you* personalized his query even more.

"I don't mind that she returned the clothes, Chris. Ellicott's is doing brisk business." She shifted her position in bed, propping herself up against the wealth of throw pillows as she lay atop her jacquard comforter.

"That's fine, Eliza. But we both know I'm not talking about that."

She swallowed. He was speaking about the attraction simmering between them like a pot left too long on a hot stove. "I know what you're talking about, Chris. I'm just…not sure how to answer your question."

"Be honest, Eliza. Just be true to what you feel."

She sighed. At one point in her life, she'd longed

for a second chance with Chris. Back then, she'd been idealistic enough to think that if they just gave it another shot, things could work out between them, and they could find happiness together. She'd held on to that dream for a long time.

But that had been so many years ago. Life had shown her that things often didn't go as planned, especially when it came to relationships.

"Don't you think that what we had was special enough to deserve a second chance?" He asked the question as if there were an easy answer.

"I guess it's possible. But we're both so different now." The Chris she'd known had been the bright young man who loved skateboarding and chess and had dreams of becoming a world-famous architect. The Chris she'd run into at Prescott George a few days ago seemed very far removed from the version she'd known. He'd always been a little on the serious side, but she couldn't recall him ever being as intense and focused as he seemed now. *Am I really interested in Chris, or just in the Chris I remember from all those years ago?* When she asked herself that question, she wasn't sure of the answer.

"I really enjoyed your company. You can't blame a guy for trying."

She supposed she couldn't. But her fear of getting involved with Chris now, and exposing herself to the same heartbreak he'd dealt her back in the day, plagued her. He really did seem oblivious to the pain he'd caused her when he walked away from her. She thought of telling him about it, but saw no reason to expose her wounds to him.

In response to her silence, he said, "I promised I wouldn't pressure you, and I'm a man of my word. Do you think we can at least be friends?"

"Maybe." It was the best she could do. She didn't know if she could be "just friends" with him. It seemed impractical, considering how strong her memories were of their prior relationship. She could still recall his kiss and his touch as if they'd happened yesterday. That was another little tidbit she thought best to keep to herself.

"I really miss the talks we used to have. Do you remember? We used to talk for hours, about everything and nothing."

"Of course I remember." How could she forget? She'd poured out her heart to him, allowing him access to her secrets, her hopes and her dreams. "I told you things I'm sure I've never told anyone else."

"See? That's proof that we've got a solid basis for a friendship." His hopeful tone made Eliza's heart thud in her chest.

She rolled over onto her stomach on the bed.

"All right. I guess we can give the friendship thing a try."

"Great." He sounded pleased. "I know this great little spot in Old Town where we can grab dinner. Are you game?"

She stared at her carpet, wondering what he was playing at. "This wouldn't be a date, right?"

"Nope, no date. Just a friendly outing between friends. You know, tortillas, margaritas and good conversation."

She turned the idea over in her mind. "I do love a good margarita."

"All you gotta do is say yes."

She chuckled at the chiding in his words. "Ok. Where are we going?"

"You know that little cantina on Juan Street? Next to the beauty salon?"

She rolled her eyes upward in thought. Thinking she remembered the place, she asked, "The one with the courtyard strung with all those Christmas lights? It has those tables with the red-and-orange umbrellas, right?"

"That's the place. Can you meet me there Thursday night, around seven thirty?"

"Sure."

"Great." He was smiling, she could hear it in his voice. "I'll see you then. Good night, Eliza."

"Good night."

After she disconnected the call, she turned over onto her back and stared up at the ceiling of her bedroom. In a matter of days, she'd gone from avoiding Chris at all costs to going out with him. And now she was about to go out with him for the second time in a week.

She had no idea why or how all this was happening or how it would turn out. All she knew was that Christopher Marland possessed a unique power over her. He'd been her first love, and she'd always heard people talk about how powerful first love could be. Now she knew firsthand.

She blew out a breath. *I've got two more days to get myself together and build up my defenses before I see him again.*

She could only hope that would be enough time. Because if she fell under his spell again, and he broke her heart, she didn't know if she'd ever recover.

## Chapter 5

Thursday night, Chris arrived at the cantina around seven. The restaurant, an Old Town favorite for authentic Mexican cuisine, bustled with activity during dinner hours most nights. He'd left his drafting table as early as he could, changed into a pair of black slacks and a short-sleeved gray button-down, and headed out. He'd hoped arriving a little early would raise his chances of snagging a great table in the courtyard.

Luck was on his side, because he managed to get a table near the outer edge of the courtyard, where it bordered the neighboring plaza. The plaza, complete with a wide brick pathway and a raised stage, hosted live entertainment each night. From the table he'd chosen, not only would they have a great view of the stage, but they could also enjoy the blooming flowers and trickling fountain nearby.

When the waiter came by, he asked only for ice water. He didn't want to order without Eliza, and she wasn't due to arrive for another few minutes. With the frosty glass in hand, he took in the sights and sounds around him. The courtyard garden boasted many large, colorful flowers, as well as neatly trimmed shrubbery and carefully placed sculptures. Looking around the space, he saw couples, families and groups of friends clustered around the other tables. Lively conversation, laughter and the clinking of glasses came from every direction.

The breeze wafting through the courtyard changed direction then, bringing with it a sweet and familiar scent. He turned toward the back door of the restaurant in time to see Eliza walk inside and stop to glance around.

She wore a crisp, sleeveless yellow blouse and a pair of denim shorts. The outfit, while appropriately casual, still highlighted the soft curves of her bustline and hips. Her bare legs seemed to go on forever, stopping only where they were capped by her metallic gold sandals.

His gaze swept back up to her face. She wore very subtle makeup, and he was most intrigued by the shimmery golden gloss on her lips. Gold hoops rested in her ears, and her dark hair was brushed back to reveal her delicate features.

She spotted him then and waved. He waved back, marveling at the sexiness of her walk as she moved in his direction. He drew a deep breath, reminding himself that this wasn't supposed to be a date. It was supposed to be an evening of friendly conversation over margaritas. The closer she got to the table, the more he worried that he wouldn't be able to stick to the original plan.

"Hi, Chris." She smiled as she approached the table. "Have you been here long?"

"No." He stood and pulled out her chair. "I'm just glad I got here in time to get us a good table."

She sat down, hanging the strap of her handbag over the back of the chair. "This is a pretty great seat. I saw on the board in front that a mariachi fusion band is playing tonight."

"Yes, and I hear the band is really good." He took a long draw from his water glass. It quenched his thirst for liquid, but not his thirst for the woman sitting across from him. "The waiter left us a couple of menus. I haven't ordered, but I know what I want."

She looked at him then, squinting a little as she picked up a brightly colored laminated menu.

Her expression made him think she'd noticed the double meaning in his statement.

Silently, she turned her attention to the menu.

The waiter reappeared, and after he'd taken their order and gone back inside the cantina, Chris cleared his throat. "So, how were things at the boutique today?"

"Pretty quiet, actually. We spent a lot of time doing inventory and marking down the few spring items we still have in the store. Once they're on the clearance rack, they usually move fast."

"You know Jojo is still going to want to hear about it whenever you get new merchandise in."

She nodded. "I still plan to keep her in the loop."

"Great, I appreciate that."

"No problem." She draped one long leg over the other. "What about you? How was your day?"

"I spent the entire day at my drafting table, adjusting the plans for my latest project." He'd barely left his office all day, having spent six hours working on his sketch. "It's a new museum that will be built mostly with green and recycled materials."

Her expression changed, indicating she was impressed. "That sounds really interesting. Tell me more about what that means."

He spent a few moments telling her about the museum, the same way he'd told her brother the previous week. "I'm really glad I got the project, because I love a challenge."

Her eyebrow hitched. "Oh, really."

He nodded. "Yes. And I never back down from one."

The food and drinks came then, and conversation ceased for a few moments, replaced by the sound of sizzling coming from the cast-iron skillet holding Eliza's fajitas. As she reached for the container of tortillas, Chris dug into his own tacos.

A few bites of fajita later, she raised her margarita glass and took a sip. She smiled as she set the glass down. "That's good."

He chuckled. "You know, when we used to go out back in the day, you weren't even old enough to drink."

After another sip, she said, "I know. I was kind of young back then, but at the time I didn't feel that way. I thought of myself as an adult, you know?"

"I get it. And trust me, I thought of you as an adult, too." He winked.

The slightest shade of red filled her cheeks, just enough for him to see it. "All right, Chris. Don't start with me." Even though she chastised him, her tone remained light and playful.

"What?" He feigned innocence.

"Oh, please. I know what you're getting at." She forked up a bit of rice and raised it to her lips. "Besides, we never did anything other than make out."

"I know." He'd desired her then, and still did now. But their relationship had been chaste, and he knew that was for the best. The five-year age difference between them made him a bit more experienced in physical intimacy. While he'd wanted her, he wasn't the kind of guy to take advantage of her. "Colonel Ellicott would have probably filleted me if I'd tried anything, anyway."

She giggled. "My dad was something of a hardass, wasn't he? He was just being protective of me, though."

Chris finished his food and pushed the empty plate aside. He turned his attention to the stage and watched the activity as the night's entertainment began setting up for their performance.

Wiping her mouth with a napkin, she set down her fork. "I'm stuffed. This was really great. Just what I needed after a busy few days at the boutique."

He smiled her way. "See? A friendly dinner with me was a good idea." He saw the way she sat back in her chair, the smile on her face and the twinkle in her eye. It made him feel good to see that she'd relaxed in his presence, because he always felt comfortable with her.

The members of the mariachi band took their places on the stage, and began playing the classic Mexican folk tune "La Bamba." Chris bobbed his head to the familiar beat, and when he looked Eliza's way, he saw her tapping her foot in time.

He saw an excellent opportunity before him, and he knew he had to take it. So he took a deep breath and prepared to go out on the proverbial limb.

"Would you like to dance, Eliza?"

Eliza swallowed. Did he really just ask that question, or had it all been in her head? "Sorry, Chris, what did you just say?"

He chuckled. "I asked if you'd like to dance. The band is pretty good, and I see you tapping your foot, so…" His words trailed off.

She looked down at her tapping foot, then back up at him. Parts of her knew that if she danced with him, she'd likely be conjuring up the feelings she'd worked so hard to dismiss all these years. But Chris was right. The band was good, and she was caught up in the celebratory spirit of the music.

Letting a smile tilt her lips, she nodded. "Sure. Let's dance."

He smiled as well, as if delighted that she'd accepted his invitation. He stood and reached out to her. She placed her hand in his and let him lead her into the courtyard fronting the stage.

A few other couples were already there dancing, so they eased into an empty spot. The song, with its upbeat tempo and catchy lyrics, made Eliza feel relaxed and comfortable as she shimmied around the courtyard. She found herself singing along and heard Chris singing as well. Caught up in the nostalgia of the tune and the freedom of the moment, she couldn't stop smiling. As she danced around, her sandaled feet gliding over the aged bricks beneath them, her mood was lighter than it had been in weeks. When she looked at Chris, dancing across from her, he looked similarly chill.

This was the first time Eliza had been at the cantina in the evening, and the lights strung overhead lit up in contrast to the darkened sky seemed almost magical. The blooming flowers and greenery surrounding the courtyard made it seem like an oasis, smack-dab in the middle of one of San Diego's busiest districts. With the band playing and the two singers harmonizing the lyrics of the familiar song, the place seemed to be a world all its own. Eliza honestly couldn't think of anyone she would rather enjoy this place with than her first love.

She shook off that old nostalgia for the moment and tried to focus instead on the moment at hand.

The band switched to a midtempo song, and Eliza found herself moving a little closer to Chris. If his grin were any indication, he didn't seem to mind their proximity. She moved her arms in time with the music, letting her hips sway, and the stress of the workweek seemed to melt away.

Snapping his fingers as he moved his feet in time, he said, "See? I knew you'd enjoy this place."

She nodded. "You were right." She loved her work at the boutique, because it allowed her to indulge her passion for fashion. Still, there were times when the business side of things overwhelmed her and encroached on the creative joy she usually experienced. Ellicott's was a small boutique, and as owner, she filled all the major leadership roles there. Invoices, purchase orders, dealing with her employees' scheduling conflicts; all those decidedly dull tasks fell under her authority. It was nice to get away from that now and then, to do something simply for personal enjoyment.

The music changed again then, but this time, the band segued smoothly into a beautiful, lilting ballad. All around the courtyard, couples embraced and began slow-dancing. The phenomenon continued until Eliza and Chris were the only two people left on the "dance floor" who had any noticeable distance between their bodies.

He held out his hand again, just as he had when he'd first invited her to dance. "May I?"

She raised her gaze to look into his sparkling dark eyes, and her heart turned a backflip inside her chest. She nodded, saying nothing. Grabbing his hand, she took two large steps that brought her into his personal space. A moment later, she felt his strong hands come to rest on her waist. As if by second nature, her arms went up around his neck, her forearms resting on the muscled expanse of his broad shoulders.

The song, relying heavily on an acoustic guitar and the impassioned vocals of a lone female singer, was as lovely as the night. Eliza didn't know much Spanish, but between the words she did understand and the longing in the vocalist's delivery, she knew just what type of song this was. A torch song. How fitting, as she stood in the arms of the only man she'd ever really loved. She let her gaze drop away from his handsome face.

They swayed back and forth together as the night breezes caressed her bare skin in the way she wished he would. Once upon a time, he had touched her that way; always chaste, yet always as sweet and sensual as a touch could ever be. She kept her eyes straight ahead, which meant looking at his collarbone. That was far better than looking into his eyes again, because she knew that if she did, she would come undone.

As the vocalist hit a particularly high note, Chris placed his bent index finger beneath her chin. Wordlessly, he tilted her face upward, effectively forcing her to look at him. He said nothing, letting the intensity of his gaze speak for him.

Eliza gasped but couldn't look away. She remembered a time when he'd had full possession of her heart, and when she looked into his coal-dark eyes, it was as if that time had never ended.

In that moment, it became clear why all her relationships had failed. Her feelings for Chris lingered on, despite their long separation. She wondered if she could ever really be free of the power he held over her, the power of first love.

Everything she'd tried to tamp down, all the feelings she'd hoped to tuck away, came to the surface like fast-rising floodwaters.

Fighting the attraction seemed silly at this point, with it hanging in the air between them like a thick fog. She wanted this, so help her. Following through on her desires, she puckered her lips and closed her eyes.

Chris bent and kissed her then. His arms slipped around her waist, pulling her closer. His lips were soft against her own, and the contact was brief and sweet, yet filled with unspoken emotion. For the time their lips were touching, there seemed to be no one else on Earth but the two of them. He used only his lips, keeping the kiss innocent. Yet the fire rising in Eliza's belly indicated her desire for something far more carnal.

He gave her a few light brushes of his lips along her jawline, then eased away.

Breathless, she opened her eyes and looked around.

It was then she realized that the song had ended. The band was on break, if their absence from the stage was any indication. Glancing nervously around, she saw that everyone else had already cleared the dance floor. Beyond that, more than a few people were eyeing them curiously from their seats.

Her cheeks heated, she grasped Chris's hand and they dashed back to their table.

## Chapter 6

Chris crossed the grassy expanse at Embarcadero Marina Park South the next evening with Eliza's hand in his own. Walking next to him, she wore a serene smile that enhanced her beauty. Seeing her so relaxed put him at ease as well, and he felt good knowing he'd played a role in her current mood.

As they approached the area bordering the bay where the stage and seating had been set up for tonight's outdoor concert, he drew in a deep breath of fresh air. The evening breeze coming off the water perfectly complemented the mild temperatures. The two of them were dressed similarly, in jeans and long-sleeved tops, and Chris felt comfortable and appropriately dressed for the weather.

The concert wasn't due to start for another half hour, and though people had already started arriving, a good number of empty seats remained. Seeing two good spots not far from the stage, he led her toward them.

"It's really nice out tonight," Eliza commented as they slid into the two chairs in the third row.

He looked out at the water, noting the way the sunlight played across the rippling surface. "I agree. Great night for the show."

"I'm glad you asked me to come."

He smiled. "I'm glad you said yes." After the two of them had left the cantina the night before, he'd asked her to come with him to tonight's concert. He'd been surprised but happy when she said yes. For the first time, she'd agreed to go without any hesitation, and he considered that a definite step in the right direction.

"I've heard a lot about Dangerous Curves." She tucked her purse beneath her seat, then looked his way. "Have you heard them perform before?"

He shook his head. "No, but I'm looking forward to it as well." His tastes in music were eclectic, and he loved hearing it performed live. "Between my work and the twins, my schedule can get pretty crazy. But I try to make time to hear live music as often as I can."

"I saw a few bands at the state fair last summer, but I haven't really been to any shows since." She brushed a windblown lock of hair out of her face.

While she chattered away about the performers she'd seen at the fair, he listened. Soon, though, he found his focus had shifted. While he knew he should be paying attention to her words, he found himself staring at her lips instead. Whatever gloss she wore gave them an appealing rosy tint. Watching her lips move as she spoke did something to him; mainly, it reminded him of the sweet kiss they'd shared last night, as well as her reaction. She'd been so pliant in his arms, one could say she'd melted against him. He assumed the kiss they'd shared was the reason she'd been so open to spending more time with him. Now that they'd acted on their lingering attraction to each other, he hoped they could put any awkwardness behind them.

They talked for a few minutes more, but fell silent as the band began its set. Dangerous Curves, a local fusion band that played a mixture of soul, blues and funk, wasted no time getting straight to the music. The all-female group included a vocalist/lead guitarist, a bassist, a drummer and a keyboardist. Kicking off the concert with an updated cover of the classic Gap Band track "Early in the Morning," the ladies had no trouble getting the crowd moving.

Chris watched Eliza as she got on her feet, swaying in time with the music. He loved seeing her this relaxed in his presence; it was something he hadn't seen in years. Soon he got up as well and joined in her dancing.

Things remained that way throughout the show, as they danced, laughed and enjoyed each other's company. The entire set was upbeat, with all the songs ranging from midtempo to fast, so there were no awkward pauses leading up to a slow dance. By the time the show ended, well after sunset, Chris felt a little sweaty from all the activity, but still fortunate to be in Eliza's company.

As they walked hand in hand to his car, she said, "Wow. Live music two nights in a row. This has been really great."

He smiled. "I'm glad you're enjoying yourself."

"It's really been too long since I've done this sort of thing." She sighed, looking off toward the water. "Burton would never have taken me to shows like this. He only listened to classical music. I mean, I like classical, too, but there's only so many times I'm gonna go to the symphony."

He felt his brow crease. "Who's Burton?"

She looked back his way. "Oh, sorry. Burton Brown is my ex-boyfriend. We dated when I was in New York. He's a lawyer, super serious and stuffy."

"A stuffy guy who would only take you to the symphony? Sounds like a fun guy at parties."

She chuckled. "Parties. Yet another place he wouldn't be caught dead."

Chris shook his head. "How long were you involved with that guy?"

She shrugged. "About eight months. Finally, I got tired of dealing with him, especially since I knew there was no future in it. Anyway, I came home and opened my store right after we broke up, so I guess he was something of a catalyst for me to get to where I am now."

He nodded. *Not only is this guy dull, he's also an idiot for not fighting to keep a woman like Eliza.*

"But enough about Burton the boring. What about you? Have you been in any relationships recently?" She asked the question as they approached his car.

He shook his head, swinging open the passenger-side door for her. "Nah. With the kids, and work, and Prescott George stuff, my plate is pretty full." He closed her inside, then went around and climbed into the driver's seat.

When he'd buckled up and looked her way, he found her watching him. "What is it?"

"It sounds like you were saying you're too busy for a relationship." Her eyes locked with his. "That doesn't really make sense to me."

"Being busy is only part of the equation." He started the engine, put the car in gear and backed out of the parking space. Joining the line of cars waiting to get out of the parking lot, he continued, "I'm also very cautious about the people I allow into my life. My relationship with Sheila taught me to be careful when choosing who I interact with. So you also have to know that there was never a woman I crossed paths with who seemed right for me."

"So you're saying there wasn't anyone you felt was worth pursuing?"

"No." He shook his head, amused at the way she kept dissecting and analyzing his words. With the car idling in the line, he turned to look directly at her. "Until now."

Redness seeped into her cheeks, and she looked away. "Goodness, Chris."

He shrugged. "It's the truth, Eliza."

The line began to move, and soon they were back on the road, headed to Ellicott's, where he'd picked her up earlier. When he parked, he hopped out to open her door.

She shook her head as he helped her out. "You're really something, Chris. Not a lot of true gentlemen left these days."

"Just treating you the way you deserve to be treated."

They walked a few steps to her car. Once she was inside, he commented, "You know, I'm willing to pick you up at home." He had no idea where she'd been living since she returned to San Diego, and he sensed she didn't want him to know. He couldn't imagine why, but didn't want to press the issue.

"I know. And you will…eventually. Good night, Chris."

"Good night, Eliza."

She winked as she started her car. As he stepped up on the sidewalk, she pulled away.

Rolling her merchandise cart out of the stockroom at Ellicott's, Eliza took care to navigate around the counter. The store was quiet for a Saturday morning, and she'd decided to use the lull to her advantage by changing out her clearance displays.

As she rolled around the counter and down the

center aisle, she passed Coretta Sinclair, her store manager. A sweet, no-nonsense woman in her mid-forties, Coretta had a husband and two grown sons. Seated on a low stool to the right of the center aisle, Coretta busied herself by dressing the full-body mannequin lying across her lap. "What do you think, Eliza?"

Bringing the cart to a halt, Eliza looked over the outfit on the mannequin. "It's great. The colors are complementary, without being too match-y. I think it will definitely help us move some of the transition fall collection."

Coretta nodded. "Good. I'm thinking I'll add some jewelry to it. Any suggestions?"

Mentally cataloging the jewelry she had on hand, Eliza thought for a moment before responding. "I'd say the light blue rock crystal set from Rainfall Designs."

"Sounds perfect." Setting the mannequin aside, Coretta ran off to grab the jewelry. When she returned, she added the necklace and bracelet before placing the mannequin on its round acrylic pedestal. "Our girl looks pretty good, don't you think?"

Eliza giggled. The staff frequently referred to the mannequins as "the girls." "Yes. She's ready."

They worked together on changing out some of the older displays, and Eliza pulled some of the spring clearance items that hadn't yet sold down and placed them in the cart. Her policy was to donate items that remained in the store for more than four months, which helped the less fortunate in the community and helped to keep her selection as fresh as possible.

The satellite station playing over the store's speakers began broadcasting the Gap Band's "You Dropped a Bomb on Me," and Eliza found herself tapping her foot to the rhythm. "I wish the band had performed this yesterday." She didn't realize she'd spoken her thoughts until Coretta responded.

Easing closer to her, Coretta gasped. "You saw the Gap Band in concert and didn't invite me?"

Eliza shook her head. "I wouldn't do you like that. I went to a show last night of a local cover band, and hearing the Gap Band reminded me of the show." She could feel the smile tilting her lips as she recalled her evening of fun…and her handsome escort. "Chris and I had a great time."

Brow raised, Coretta eyed her. "Chris? Not the same Chris whose ex-wife came in here last week causing a ruckus, right?"

She pursed her lips. "Yes, the same Chris. How many men do you think I see in a week?"

"Usually none, but that's beside the point." Coretta folded a graphic T-shirt and placed it on the stack with its mates. "I'm guessing you and Chris have...history."

She nodded. "We do." She left out that Chris was her first love, and that she'd never really had any strong feelings for anyone else. *No need to divulge all my business.* "He was a perfect gentleman, and I really enjoyed his company."

Coretta's expression changed, but she pursed her lips shut.

Eliza sensed the unspoken words piling up in Coretta's mouth. "What do you want to say? Because I can tell it's killing you to hold it back."

"I was just going to say you should be careful if you're thinking of getting involved with Chris."

She already knew that, but didn't say so. She wanted to hear Coretta's reasoning, so she asked, "What makes you say that?"

"He's divorced. Not only that, he has children." Adding another folded T-shirt to the stack, she continued. "You know Arthur is my second husband. My first husband Elbert is the father of my sons. After we split up, Elbert made it his mission to keep me single."

Eliza could feel the tension building in her shoulders. Reaching up to lightly massage the areas, she sighed. "We're not involved, Coretta. He's just a part of my past that's resurfaced."

"You're not involved, yet. But I saw the way you smiled when you talked about him. It's only a matter of time before this thing turns into a full-on courtship."

Not knowing how to feel about that, Eliza ran a hand over her hair. She looked to the door, hoping a customer would walk in at that moment and rescue her from the uncomfortable realities of this conversation.

No such respite came, and Coretta kept talking. "I'm not trying to tell you what to do. After all, I'm much too young to be your mama. But his ex has already shown you that she's petty by showing up here to make a fuss about the things he bought their daughter. So just be cautious. That's all I'm saying."

"I will." When it came to Chris, she had no choice but to proceed with care. He had such a hold over her, she knew she'd have to work to protect herself from another heartbreak at his hands. "On the bright side, his daughter does like me. I think she referred to me as 'cool.'"

Coretta grinned. "That is a point in your favor."

The bell over the door rang, and two ladies entered the store. As Coretta set aside the bin of T-shirts to wait on them, Eliza took a deep breath. Coretta had given her a lot to mull over, as if she weren't already overanalyzing the situation between her and Chris. Now she had even more to think about.

Chris had a full, busy life; he'd said so himself. He had his children, his design work and his work with Prescott George all vying for his time and attention. That didn't even take his dealings with his ex-wife into account. Eliza could tell her old feelings for Chris were resurfacing. What she couldn't see was where she fit into his already packed life.

Could he really have the time, space and freedom to let her into his heart?

Or would she fall by the wayside in favor of his other commitments?

# Chapter 7

Chris looked around the crowded gymnasium of Valley Arts Academy, searching the teeming mass of teenagers for the two that belonged to him. He'd arrived at the dance with Jack and Jojo less than half an hour ago, and they'd already made themselves scarce. He wasn't really surprised by their disappearing act; they'd been doing that for about two years now. He guessed that was the age when kids discovered their parents didn't know everything after all, and began thinking of them as "uncool."

He spotted Jojo then, partly by the bright color

of her orange dress. After Jojo had refused to attend the dance unless she could have the dress she'd chosen, Chris and Sheila had reached a compromise. Sheila had agreed to let Jojo have the dress she wanted on the condition that she not be left out of her daughter's wardrobe decisions for any future dances. He'd repurchased Jojo's favorite dress from Ellicott's, and tonight she looked lovely, albeit far more grown-up than he would have expected.

He walked over to where she stood, chatting with two friends from her class. He waved at the other girls, then gently took his daughter by the hand. "Jojo, I've been looking for you."

"What is it, Dad?"

"Can I talk to you for a minute?"

She eyed her friends, who could barely hide their curious expressions. "Can't it wait 'til later?"

He shook his head. "Sorry, kiddo, it can't wait. I promise you'll be back with your friends in a flash."

"Okay." She acquiesced, letting him lead her toward the plastic-covered table that served as the punch station. Once there, she looked up at him. "What's up?"

"We didn't really get to talk before the dance, so I just wanted to talk about tonight."

She sighed. "How come you didn't talk to me about this in the car, after you picked me and Jack up?"

He chuckled. "Both your faces were buried in your phones. I didn't think you'd be listening." He gave her hand a squeeze. "Besides, I wanted to talk to just you. Jack doesn't really need to hear what I have to say."

She slipped her hand out of his, propped her bare shoulder against the wall. "Okay, Dad."

"I want to make sure you understand the ways you should behave tonight. This is your first dance, and I…"

Jojo let her head drop back, rolling her eyes. "Dad. Geez."

He couldn't hold back his smirk at her combination of embarrassment and exasperation. "Ground rules, Jojo. Make sure you get your own punch, and don't finish it if it tastes funny. Don't leave the gym without letting me know. And if you're going to dance with boys…"

"I know, I know. Keep a full arm's length of distance between us." She blew out a breath, folded her arms over her chest. "Dad, you told me all this before. Can I go now?"

He could see her expression and her body language; she wanted to get back to her friends. "Yes,

Jojo. Just remember what I told you. And if anybody gives you any trouble, come and tell me right away, okay?"

"I will, Dad." She dropped her arms. "So far, no one's given me any trouble but you." She pursed her lips playfully.

He shooed her away. "Go on back to your friends. I'm sure you don't want to miss out on any more gossip."

She scurried away then, rejoining the two girls she'd been talking to. He watched them chatter for a few moments, gesturing and laughing. Soon, though, all three of them were looking down, eyes glued to their phones. He shook his head, knowing they'd probably started texting one another. He'd seen them do it before, even as they all sat next to one another on Sheila's couch.

He moved away from the punch table, closer to the small stage that had been set up in the front of the gym for the DJ. In a corner to the left of the stage, he spotted Jack, sitting at a table with his debate team buddies. Just like Jojo and her girlfriends, all the young men around the table were staring at their phones.

He wanted to groan, but he knew better than to judge them. He spent his fair share of time on his own smartphone, and because of his workload, there wasn't any getting around that. He could imagine plenty of the other kids' parents were similarly tethered to their devices. He really didn't have to imagine, because when he looked around at the other chaperones posted in various spots around the gym, he saw most of them looking down, their faces illuminated by their glowing screens. In a way, the kids were probably just mimicking what they saw at home.

He went back to his station by the snack table, thinking about the high school dances he'd attended. He remembered those awkward gatherings in ninth and tenth grade, where boys and girls would stand on opposites sides of the gym, watching each other. They'd remain that way for an hour or more, until one brave soul left the boys' side to ask a girl to dance. If she shot him down, he would likely leave rather than slink back to his boys wearing the stench of defeat. If she agreed, the rest would soon pair off and fill the dance floor.

Something similar was happening now in Valley's gym. Most of the boys were on one side of the gym, while the girls held court on the other. The presence of smart devices and the music made the scene a little different, but Chris could see that the fragile, uncertain interactions between boys and girls of this age were still just as complex as they'd been twenty-odd years ago.

As the night wore on, Chris helped himself to a few snacks and a cool glass of punch. The dance floor filled up during songs with popular dances that the kids all seemed to know. He could remember doing the Electric Slide at a few dances back in the day, and though the current line dances looked different, the concept remained the same: catchy song plus easy-to-follow dance steps equaled a jam-packed dance floor.

The end of the dance drawing near, Chris watched the kids shuffle toward the sidelines as the DJ put on a slow record. Out of the corner of his eye, he saw a young man approaching Jojo. Turning in that direction, he discreetly watched their interaction. The young man leaned close to Jojo's ear and spoke to her, after which she blushed and nodded. Chris watched as the boy led Jojo away from her grinning girlfriends and out on the dance floor.

"That's Anthony Jordan," a voice beside Chris announced. "Jojo's got a huge crush on him."

Chris shifted his attention toward the voice and saw his son Jack standing next to him. "Jack, what do you know about this guy?"

Jack shrugged. "He plays on the basketball

team, I think. I know he's in chess club, and he pretty much keeps to himself when he's not on the court or playing chess."

Chris drew a deep breath. Young Jordan sounded like he was on the up and up. "What grade is he in? How old is he?"

"Dad, I don't know him like that. He's in tenth grade, but that's all I got for you." Jack took a sip from the paper cup of punch in his hand. "What do you want me to do, take his fingerprints or something? Maybe get a blood sample?"

"That won't be necessary." He chuckled at his son's offer. Jack's dry sense of humor and penchant for sarcasm meant there was never a dull moment raising him. "What about you, Jack? Any girls out there you want to dance with?"

Another shrug. "Not really. Girls seem like a whole lot of trouble to me." He tossed his empty cup into the trash. "Oh, there's Brady. Later, Dad."

"Meet me by the front office when the dance is over," Chris called after him. "And thanks for the intel."

"No prob." Jack disappeared into the crowd.

Standing alone again, Chris looked out on the dance floor, his gaze landing on Jojo and Anthony. He smiled when he saw the wide gulf between them. Jojo's hands rested on Anthony's shoulders, while his hands were on her sides, just above the waist. She'd seemed restless and uninterested during their talk earlier, but at least she'd taken his advice to heart. And in the end, her willingness to do that would matter more than anything.

*That's my girl.*

Monday evening, Eliza strolled through one of the galleries at the San Diego Museum of Art. The current exhibition, exploring the art of the twentieth century, had many intriguing pieces. So far, the paintings had been her favorite, and as she stopped to admire one, she glanced over her shoulder. Seeing Chris lingering in front of another painting mounted a few feet away, she thought about the surprise in his voice when she'd asked him to pick her up—at home—and bring her here. Now he knew she lived in the cottage on her parents' property. He hadn't said anything about it, but she could tell by the way he'd been acting that it was on his mind.

Not wanting to overthink it, she returned her attention to the painting she'd stopped to look at.

As she contemplated the artwork, resisting the urge to trace her fingertips along the smooth brushstrokes imprinted in the oil paint, she wondered what the artist's process was like. She didn't consider herself a creative person, though she had to tap into that side of herself to design displays at her boutique. And while she loved the thrill of setting up a display that caught the attention of her customers, she saw little connection between that and the talent and skill displayed in the painting.

Her mind switched gears when he entered her space. She felt his presence even before he moved behind her to slip his arms around her waist. Her body responded to his touch, every nerve ending seemed to tingle with the electricity of his nearness.

She turned in the circle of his arms, pecked him on the cheek and slipped out of his grasp. "Chris, not here."

"What's the matter?"

She leaned in, whispering in his ear. "Put the kibosh on the PDA, will you? At least until we leave the gallery."

He smiled. "As you wish, Eliza."

Rolling her eyes at his silliness, she started walking again.

He followed, shortening his long stride to walk next to her. "What did you do over the weekend? I mean, besides working at the boutique."

She shrugged. "Not much, really. I was either

at the store or at home catching up on my shows all weekend. How about you? Anything exciting?"

He chuckled. "In a way. This was my weekend with the kids. The arrangement I have with my ex is to get them every other weekend."

"Did you and the twins do anything fun?"

"They did. The school dance was Saturday night. I came back to the store to pick up Jojo's dress that morning, but your manager said you'd gone on coffee break." He paused by another painting. "Anyway, I chaperoned the dance."

"Sounds like fun."

"For the kids, maybe. For me it was somewhat dull, but I liked being there to keep an eye on them."

They found a low bench just outside the gallery and took a seat. While Chris recounted the happenings of the school dance, Eliza listened. Hearing the way he spoke about the twins and seeing the expression on his face when he mentioned their names, it was clear how much he loved his children. It must be a profound feeling, loving a child you'd helped to create. She wouldn't know, having no children of her own. One day she hoped to know the joy of motherhood, but for now, she spent as much time as she could with her nieces and nephews.

He stopped then, as if sensing how she felt. "I'm sorry, Eliza. I didn't mean to ramble on about the kids. Let's just say they keep me pretty busy."

"I'll bet they do, and it's fine. I don't mind at all." She squeezed his shoulder. "It's nice to hear you talk about them, because I can tell you love them very much."

He smiled then. "Jojo and Jack are the best and brightest things in my life. All the hard work I put in at the drafting table is really for them. I'm working to secure their future." He looked away then, chuckled. "Hopefully they'll repay me by taking care of me in my old age."

She laughed. "It's the least they could do. Then maybe you've got a shot at having someone to push your wheelchair. I just have to hope one of my sisters' kids will look after me, since I don't have any of my own."

"How many nieces and nephews do you have? Vaughn's told me, but I've forgotten."

"We've got three nieces and two nephews, between our two sisters." She gave their names and ages. "The oldest is about to start high school in the fall, and the youngest is still a year away from preschool, so quite an age range."

"Do you babysit them?"

"Sometimes. But never all five at once." She

giggled. "I love them, but I don't want to be out-numbered and overpowered, you know?"

"I get it. Five kids and one adult is a little risky. You could have mutiny on your hands." He winked.

She felt her heart flutter in her chest. How could a man be this handsome? There had to be some law against it, yet here he was, out in public being gorgeous. His dark eyes settled on her face, and she felt so overwhelmed by his attention, she had to look away for a moment.

"What's the matter?" He asked the question in such a casual tone, one would think him unaware of the effect he had on her.

She cleared her throat. "Nothing. I... It's just a little hard to think when you look at me like that."

A smile stretched his lips. "Oh, really?"

She heard the teasing in his tone. Balling up her fist, she popped him playfully on the shoulder. "Quit it, Chris, or else."

"Or else what?"

She gave him her most serious look.

"Well, I see some things haven't changed. You're still a piece of work." He grabbed her hand, gave it a squeeze. "I'll try not to set you off, even though you're kind of cute when you're mad."

She pursed her lips. "Don't make me box your ears."

He stood, pulling her up with him. "There are a lot of things I want you to do to me. But that's not one of them."

She cut her eyes at him, but didn't say anything. *If only you knew how much I'd like to explore that notion.*

Leaning closer to her, he said softly, "I want to kiss you, Eliza."

Meeting his eyes, she said nothing, but gave him a small nod to indicate her willingness. As she turned her face toward him and tilted up, he lowered his lips to hers. Again, he kept the contact chaste, and again, she felt the rising heat warming her insides. He brushed his soft lips against hers several times, lingering at the last pass as she marveled at the sweetness of his kiss. When he eased away, she passed her tongue over her lower lip.

"Have I smoothed things over between us, Eliza?" His voice dragged her back to reality.

She answered truthfully. "Yes, you have." Who could be annoyed after a kiss like that? She certainly couldn't.

"Good." He gestured toward the exit. "We can go, if you're ready. Would you like to go get some ice cream?"

"Homemade?"

He scoffed. "Is there any other kind?"

She let her smile show through. "Sounds good."

"Great. I know just the place."

## Chapter 8

Chris sat at the small wrought iron table in front of the Gaslamp Creamery, a waffle cone of fudge ripple in hand. Eliza sat across from him with a dish of strawberry ice cream. There were only two other people there, a mother and daughter, sitting a few tables away. The sky had darkened, with the setting sun yielding to the coming night. The air felt as cool and light as his mood.

He watched her, noting the delicate way she raised the plastic spoon to her mouth and the soft smile that touched her lips as she enjoyed the cool, creamy treat. A breeze blew by, lifting the tendrils of her hair as she ate.

*She's so beautiful.* He'd spent the last hour and a half walking through an art gallery with her. The place had been filled with priceless works of art, sculptures and paintings by renowned artists from all over the world. Yet nothing he'd seen there could ever compare to her graceful beauty. When he looked at her, he could still see remnants of the young woman he'd fallen in love with, lying just beneath the accomplished, self-assured woman she'd become.

She cleared her throat. "Chris, is something wrong?"

"No, why do you ask?"

She tilted her head slightly to the right. "Because you're staring at me."

He averted his eyes. "Sorry about that. It's just that the way you eat ice cream is…well…kind of cute."

Her brow creased. "Cute? Hmmm. Haven't been called that in a while."

"I didn't mean to make you uncomfortable, though." He didn't know if he could stop watching her, but at least he would try to be more discreet about it.

"No biggie." She picked up her spoon again.

He shifted his focus back to his rapidly melting cone. He bit off a few chunks of sweet, crispy waffle cone, following that with a few mouthfuls of the rich, cool ice cream. It seemed like ages since he'd had a good fudge ripple, and soon, enjoyment got the better of him. Before he knew it, he'd polished off his entire cone. Feeling a dribble running from the corner of his mouth, he reached for the napkin holder in the center of the table.

It was then he noticed Eliza staring at him.

Her mouth formed a small O shape. She'd stopped eating her ice cream, and the plastic spoon dangled in her grasp above her dish, seemingly forgotten.

He chuckled, and the sound seemed to snap her out of her trance. "Now you're staring at me, Eliza."

She blinked a few times, dug her spoon into the last bit of ice cream remaining in her dish. "Sorry."

"So, why were you staring at me?" He tried, but failed, to keep the teasing tone out of his question.

With a sidelong glance, she replied, "There's something about the way you devoured that cone. It was…" She let the sentence trail off.

"Cute?" He ventured to complete her sentence with the same word he'd used to describe her earlier.

She shook her head. "Cute is definitely not the

word I would use." Her expression changed then, and she swirled the spoon around in a pool of melted ice cream. "Let's just say I was—intrigued."

He didn't know what she meant by that, because he couldn't think of anything particularly interesting about the way he'd eaten the ice cream cone. It had probably been too fast, and maybe a little messy, but not entertaining, at least to his mind. Despite his confusion, he decided not to question her further. From her expression, he couldn't tell whether she was annoyed to be caught staring at him or had simply grown bored of his company for the night. He used to think himself an expert on all things Eliza Ellicott. There'd been a time when he'd been able to guess her thoughts, say things that made her smile and finish her sentences... correctly. But if he were honest with himself, that was a long time ago. Maybe he didn't know her as well as he thought he did, at least not this current, older version of her.

When the silence dragged on a little too long for his tastes, he asked, "Are you ready to go?"

She nodded. "Sure."

They got up from the table, discarding their trash in the bin by the door, and headed for his car parked nearby.

As he held open the door for her, he commented,

"I don't want to keep you out too late, or the Colonel will be after me." He could recall many nights he'd had to deal with Eliza's father, when they'd stayed out later than he preferred. The Colonel had retired from the military ages ago, but he still had a lot of toughness in him, especially when it came to his daughter.

She didn't respond, but he noticed her frown as he closed her inside the car.

He slipped into the driver's seat, buckled up and got on the road. She remained silent for most of the ride, and he wondered what he'd said or done to make her withdraw. He knew better than to force conversation with her, so he followed her lead and kept quiet.

He drove up the long, winding driveway at the Ellicott estate, passing by the sprawling main house and continuing until he reached the cottage Eliza called home. Of course, what the Ellicotts considered a "cottage" was actually a two-story brick structure with a screened sitting porch and an attached one-car garage.

Pulling up in front of the garage door, he cut the engine. He reached to undo his seat belt, intent on getting out and opening the door for her. To his surprise, she unlatched her belt, tossed it aside and opened her door.

By the time he made it around to the passenger side, she'd already climbed out. Clutching her purse, she strode toward the porch.

After closing the door she'd left standing open, he followed her. "What's wrong, Eliza?"

"Nothing." She didn't look at him, instead concentrating on jamming her key into the lock.

He frowned. *What's going on with her?* "Listen, if I said or did something that rubbed you the wrong way, I'm sorry."

She turned the knob and pushed the front door open. Turning her expressionless face his way, she said flatly, "I'm fine. I'm really tired and I need to get to bed. Good night, Chris."

He leaned in for a kiss, and she jerked her head, allowing him only a peck on her cheek. Stepping back, he wished her good night, then watched her disappear inside, closing the door behind her.

He stood on the porch for a few moments, wondering what had just happened. Then, with a sigh, he returned to his car.

Tuesday evening, Eliza lay stretched out on the sofa in the living room of her cottage. She'd stopped off for a salad on the way home from Ellicott's, and now enjoyed the quiet and solitude of her space. Situated about a half mile from her par-

ents' home, the cottage had two levels, and included two bedrooms and one and a half baths,
giving her more than enough room to spread out.
It had been a busy day at the store, and she propped
her feet up on the arm of the sofa. They needed the
rest, because she'd been on her feet for nine hours.

The television was on, showing an episode of
*Julia*, the groundbreaking late-sixties sitcom. Lead
actress Diahann Carroll was the first black actress to have a sitcom where she didn't portray a
stereotypical role, such as a maid. Eliza's mother,
Natalie, had raved about the show, and Eliza tried
to catch the reruns when she could. Diahann had
a gift for humorous delivery of her lines, and her
son, Corey, played by actor Marc Copage, was
about as cute and endearing as a kid could be.

A commercial break began, and her mind
drifted back to her evening with Chris. She
couldn't believe how he'd related to her. Calling
her "cute" and bringing up her father, as if she
were still a teenager. His comments had annoyed
her to no end, and he'd seemed oblivious to his
error. Here she was, an adult with a successful
business, and he still seemed to think of her as
that idealistic nineteen-year-old. She'd been eager
to get away from him, because it was either that
or read him the riot act.

Halfway through the episode, Eliza's phone rang. She shifted on the couch so she could reach the buzzing device. Grabbing it from the coffee table, she answered it. "Hello?"

"Hey sis, it's Brianne."

She smiled. "Hey, Bri. What's up with you?"

She scoffed. "Girl, you know ain't nothing exciting happening here. With three kids running around here, I pretty much only leave the house to get groceries and run errands."

"Right. But you know you love them."

"Of course I do. So, what's going on with you?"

Eliza put the phone on speaker, so she could get back into her comfortable position. "Let's see. I sold five dresses to a lady planning a casual outdoor wedding. She said she wanted something cute and breezy, and not too stuffy for her venue on the bay. After that, I packed up the last of the spring inventory and sent it over to the women's shelter. Then I…"

Brianne cut her off. "Girl. I ask you what's up, and you give me the blow-by-blow of what happened at work?"

"What's wrong with that?"

She chuckled. "Come on, Eliza. I know you're a serious businesswoman and all, and we're all super proud of you. But you should have a social life, too. You know what they say about all work and no play."

Rolling her eyes, Eliza said, "Yeah, yeah. I know. You'll be glad to know I've been out on a few dates this past week."

In a voice laden with delight, Brianne said, "Ooooh! You got a man, girl? Tell me all the juicy details."

Eliza laughed at her sister's antics. "Bri, there's nothing juicy to tell. We've been out for Mexican food and dancing, a concert at the park and to a museum so far."

"Mmm-hmm. So, who is this guy? No man has been able to get near you since you broke up with…er…you-know-who."

It gratified Eliza that her sister knew better than to say Burton's name. "It's Chris."

"Chris who?" Brianne sounded genuinely confused. "I know at least four dudes named Chris."

She took a deep breath, fully expecting her sister to have a conniption when she heard his full name. "Chris Marland."

"What? No way!" Brianne's shout indicated her shock.

Eliza pulled the phone away from her ear. "Yes way. And can you chill with that yelling in my ear?"

"I'm sorry, girl. But damn, what did you expect? Hearing you say his name after all these years is pretty surprising." She paused, took a breath. "Okay, now break it down for me. How did this come about?"

Eliza explained her recent encounter with Chris. "Basically, if I hadn't gone by the Prescott George office looking for Vaughn, I probably wouldn't have run into him." Saying that aloud made her think about the repercussions of it. She'd been home for about a while, and she'd managed to avoid any contact with Chris up until she'd gone by the office that day.

"True. San Diego is a big city." Brianne chuckled. "Plus, there was the fact that you were purposely avoiding him."

Eliza cringed, but tried to keep her tone even as she asked, "What makes you say that?"

"Girl, please. I'm your sister, and I know you. Besides, I remember the way things went down between you and Chris back in the day, and I can understand why you wouldn't want to see him."

Eliza sat up on the sofa, letting a sigh escape. "Anyway, I've had a lot of fun with Chris over the past couple of weeks. He's still a charmer, and he's aged like expensive wine." She'd thought Chris was handsome years ago, but these days, he was fine with a capital *F*.

"So, does that mean you've patched things up with him? Are you two back together?"

"No, I wouldn't say we're back together."

Brianne chuckled. "Then what would you say you two are doing?"

She thought about it for a moment. "We're hanging out, enjoying each other's company. So much has changed over the years, so it's like getting to know each other all over again."

"Mmm-hmm." Brianne didn't sound terribly convinced. "I'm sure you know where all this 'getting to know each other' can lead. Right to the bedroom."

Eliza cracked, "Yeah, right. We're nowhere near that point, Bri." She didn't mention how much she'd like to move in that direction with Chris, because her sister was already teasing her. "Trust me, a few pecks do not constitute a relationship."

"Oh, so you've kissed him, then?"

Eliza dropped her head in her hands, realizing too late that she'd said too much. "Oh, hush, Bri. It's no big deal."

"You know me, sis. I'm not about to tell you how to live your life. But I do have one more question."

"What's that?"

"Do Vaughn and Daddy know you've been seeing Chris?"

Eliza felt her spine stiffen at the mention of her father and older brother. "No. I'm grown—I don't have to tell them everything I do."

"I know that. But when they find out, it's probably going to be a problem. You know how overprotective Daddy is over you, since you're the baby. And Vaughn's not likely to be a fan of this, either."

"But Vaughn and Chris are friends, though. Plus, they do all that work together for Prescott George, so that means they can get along."

"True. But remember, Vaughn wasn't too pleased about what went down between you and Chris, and I don't know that he's every really forgotten that."

When Eliza thought about it, she realized she didn't know, either. It was highly possible that Vaughn still held a grudge against Chris. Her brother could be incredibly stubborn, but as a businessman, he knew how to act when in a professional setting. Vaughn wasn't the type to pop off and punch a guy, but he could be prone to long-simmering anger. "Oh, crap."

"On that note, I'm getting off this phone. I've been on here long enough. I need to check on your nieces before they color on my walls or start a small fire." Brianne made a smooching sound in her ear. "Love you, sis. Talk to you later."

"Love you, too. Bye, Bri." Disconnecting the call, Eliza tried to get back into her show, but she found it hard to focus. Here she was, annoyed that Chris still saw a teenager when he looked at her. She hadn't even considered how the men in her family would react to her seeing Chris again.

For right now, she wouldn't contact Chris. If he wanted to see her, he'd have to make the effort to reach her. She figured if she made him take the initiative, he'd either start to see her as a grown woman or he'd lose interest.

Deciding not to spend any more time thinking about him right now, she got up and went to the kitchen to grab a drink. A touch of gin would be just the ticket to get Chris and his wrongheaded thinking off her mind.

# Chapter 9

Chris raised his glass of ginger ale and took a long draw. It was Wednesday, and he'd agreed to meet Vaughn at a local sandwich shop for lunch to discuss the ongoing issues facing Prescott George. He didn't often leave his home office in the middle of the day to come into the city, but with things being what they were, it was important that he and Vaughn meet to discuss their next move.

Internally, Chris wondered how Vaughn would react if Vaughn knew he was seeing Eliza again. He thought about mentioning it, but decided

Dear Reader,

***IT'S A FACT:*** if you answer 4 quick questions, we'll send you **4 FREE REWARDS!**

I'm not kidding you. As a leading publisher of women's fiction, we value your opinions... and your time. That's why we are prepared to **reward** you handsomely for completing our mini-survey. In fact, we have 4 Free Rewards for you, including 2 free books and 2 free gifts.

As you may have guessed, that's why our mini-survey is called **"4 for 4".** Answer 4 questions and get 4 Free Rewards. It's that simple!

Thank you for participating in our survey,

*Pam Powers*

## To get your 4 FREE REWARDS:
### Complete the survey below and return the insert today to receive 2 FREE BOOKS and 2 FREE GIFTS guaranteed!

# "4 for 4" MINI-SURVEY

**1** Is reading one of your favorite hobbies?
☐ YES  ☐ NO

**2** Do you prefer to read instead of watch TV?
☐ YES  ☐ NO

**3** Do you read newspapers and magazines?
☐ YES  ☐ NO

**4** Do you enjoy trying new book series with FREE BOOKS?
☐ YES  ☐ NO

**YES!** I have completed the above Mini-Survey. Please send me my 4 FREE REWARDS (worth over $20 retail). I understand that I am under no obligation to buy anything, as explained on the back of this card.

### 168/368 XDL GMYK

FIRST NAME

LAST NAME

ADDRESS

APT.#

CITY

STATE/PROV.

ZIP/POSTAL CODE

against it. There was already enough tension going on within PG, and he didn't need to add to it.

Polishing off the last of his club sandwich, Chris wiped his mouth with a napkin and tossed it aside. "So, let's talk. I've got to get back to work on my floor plans."

Vaughn nodded. "I understand. I'll have to get back over to Elite as well." He reached into an interior pocket of his sport coat, pulled out a folded piece of paper. After unfolding it, he slid it across the table. "I would have shown you this earlier, but I didn't want to ruin your appetite."

Chris picked up the newspaper clipping, his gaze naturally falling on the bolded headline. His eyes widened as he read it aloud. "Misappropriation of funds suspected at Prescott George!" He silently read the first two paragraphs of the article before slapping the paper down on the table again. "We just can't seem to catch a break."

"I know. I just can't figure out why all this bad publicity keeps coming our way. Is somebody in the chapter talking to the press?"

He shook his head. "No, not if they're following my edict. I announced weeks ago that no member of the San Diego chapter was to engage the press." Some thought he was overreacting by making such a sweeping demand, but as president of the chapter, whatever was said about his chapter, good or bad, reflected on him. "This is such a mess."

"You're telling me. I know you probably don't want to read the rest of the article, but I already did. It's quoting an anonymous source."

Chris rolled his eyes. "How convenient. That means we'll probably never know who's responsible."

Vaughn shook his head. "I'm starting to think someone has it in for us. I don't want that to be true, but at this point, I don't know what else to think." He pushed aside the remnants of his steak and cheese sandwich.

Placing his fingers to his temples, Chris massaged the area. He could feel a wicked headache coming on, and trying to figure out who might be trying to sabotage his chapter only made it worse. Then something popped into his head. "Do you remember a couple of weeks ago, when we were supposed to have lunch, and you ran out to fix something at Elite? Whatever happened with that?"

Vaughn leaned back in his chair. "Yes, I remember. That was a crazy day."

He watched Vaughn's face for a few moments, gleaning nothing from his flat expression. "So, what was the problem? And more importantly, does it have anything to do with Prescott George?"

"No. It was a material defect my manager discovered in a new shipment of wetsuits. The things were just falling apart as we took them out of the boxes. It was a mess, but it's not related to our issues at PG."

Chris released a pent-up breath. "That's a relief."

Vaughn frowned. "You know, you could show a little sympathy, man."

"Sorry. I don't mean to say it's good you had a problem at the store. I'm just relieved it's not tied in to the PG drama." He hadn't meant to come off as insensitive or uncaring about Vaughn's problem. Maybe this was why some people referred to him as "blunt" or "gruff." "I'm assuming you were able to straighten out the issue with the wetsuits, right?"

"Yeah. It took a few days, but we finally got all the defective suits shipped out, and then we got new, properly made suits in to replace them." He drained the last of his root beer, the ice rattling and clinking as he sat the empty glass down again. "Anyway, what are we going to do about all this?"

Chris knew Vaughn had shifted gears, turning the conversation back to Prescott George. "Without knowing who's leaking this information to the press, I don't know if there's any good way to put a lid on it."

"You're right. But we need to do something, and quick. We've got that party coming up."

Chris sighed. "Right." The upcoming party, which was meant to honor the San Diego chapter's designation as Chapter of the Year, was roughly three weeks away. He scratched his chin, trying to come up with something that might change the tone of the publicity the chapter had been getting as of late. "We need to do something to change the narrative. How about a community service project? We have the budget for that, right?"

Vaughn looked thoughtful for a moment. "I'm sure we do. The main issue will be deciding what we want to do and how much we will spend on it."

"Fine. Take a look at the books and brainstorm some practical projects that won't eat too much of our budget. Can you get back to me with a list and some figures in the next few days?"

He nodded. "I don't think that will be a problem."

After they paid for their meal, Vaughn headed to Elite while Chris made his way back home to his office. He'd just walked into his house when his phone vibrated in his pocket. "Hello?"

"Hey, Dad. It's Jack."

He smiled at the sound of his son's voice. "Hey, kiddo. What's up?"

"Listen. Do you think you could convince Mom to get off my back about football tryouts?"

Hearing the frustration in his son's voice, Chris became concerned. "She's started that up again?" He sat down on the white leather sofa in his sitting room.

Jack sighed. "Yes, and she's as determined as ever. I keep telling her I don't want to go out for the team, but she just doesn't seem to get it."

It pained him to know Sheila was pushing something on Jack and disregarding his feelings. "Son, how clear have you been with her that you're not interested?"

"Crystal clear. I've told her like a hundred times that I don't want to play football. I could maybe do track and field. But she's so set on me getting a football scholarship and playing pro ball, she's not hearing me."

Chris rolled his eyes. As she'd done with him so many years ago, Sheila was still trying to secure her future at the expense of someone else's choices. "I'm sorry, Jack. I don't know if I can convince her to stop bugging you. Your mother can be very…

insistent." He chose his words carefully, because he didn't bad-mouth his ex to their children, ever.

Jack was quiet for a moment. Then he asked, "Do you think she'll leave it alone if I try out and completely suck at it?"

He chuckled. "Maybe. But there's a chance she'll redouble her efforts and send you off to football camp."

He groaned. "Crap. I don't want that."

Chris thought for a moment. "I'll talk to her. I can't promise anything, but I'll see if I can convince her to abort mission on this. In the meantime, pick something else you like and sign up for that. You know, show her that you're filling your time with extracurriculars."

Jack's tone brightened as he picked up on what his father was hinting at. "Oh, I get it. I'll just sign up for something I actually like, something that happens to conflict with football season."

Chris smiled. "That's my boy."

"Thanks, Dad. I'll let you go."

"Okay, son. Love you."

Jack hesitated. "Yeah, You, too, Dad." Then he hung up.

Pocketing his phone, Chris chuckled. Sheila would probably flip when she found out Jack wasn't going to play football, but he didn't believe in forcing the kid into something he didn't want, at least not when it came to extracurriculars. When Sheila did things like this, it just reminded Chris of all the reasons they were never right for each other.

Still, she'd given him Jack and Jojo. And no matter how much he disagreed with her, he'd always be grateful to her for that.

Eliza pulled her cream-colored shawl tighter around her shoulders to fend off the chill of the breeze flowing over the harbor. She stood near the glass enclosure on the North Deck of Top of the Market, one of San Diego's finest restaurants. It was about an hour past sunset on Thursday night, and as she looked up at the star-sprinkled sky, she sighed. The night, as beautiful as any she could remember, seemed made for romance. The lovely scenery helped her put aside her unpleasant memories of their last interaction. If he could go through the trouble of setting this up, she could give him another shot. Everything would be fine, so long as he didn't bring up their age difference tonight.

Chris stood next to her, his shoulder resting against the glass. "Have you enjoyed yourself this evening, Eliza?"

She smiled. "Yes, I have." Looking his way,

she took in his handsomeness for the thousandth time. The tailored coal black suit fit him perfectly, as did the crisp royal blue shirt and solid black tie. His face sported a fresh shave, revealing the strong, angular lines of his face. To her, he looked as decadent as any of the rich desserts on the restaurant's menu.

His full lips tilted up into a smile. "Glad to hear it. I knew I was taking a risk by reserving the entire deck for us. I mean, what if you had said no? It was nonrefundable, you know." He winked.

She giggled. They'd been here for the past two hours, and she'd dined on sautéed New Bedford sea scallops and enjoyed a chilled glass of Moët. And to accompany the wonderful meal and the glorious views of sunset over the USS Midway and the North Harbor, she'd had Chris's company and conversation to make her night even more magical. "You didn't have to do all of this. I would have been fine eating in the dining room with everyone else."

"You're assuming I did this for you, but my reasoning was totally selfish." He took a step closer.

"Oh, really?" She took a step as well, entering his personal space.

He smiled. "Yes." He leaned in, placed a soft

kiss on her forehead. "I didn't want to share you with anyone."

She appreciated his tenderness, but the heat radiating through her body demanded to be satiated. "Whatever the reasoning, thank you. I've really enjoyed myself."

"I'm glad. But you should know, the evening isn't over yet."

Her eyebrows rose in surprise. "What's next, then?" Parts of her hoped he planned to take her back to his place and see where the night took them once they were truly alone.

"I'm going to take you for a drive."

It wasn't the answer she'd expected, but she didn't see any problem with that. "Okay. I'm game."

They left the restaurant and he drove her around the city and the surrounding areas, showing her some of the buildings he'd designed. The types of structures ran the gamut; he'd designed restaurants, retail spaces and even a church for one of the local Baptist congregations. She alternated between looking out the window at the places he pointed out, and squirming in her seat. Tonight, the inside of his car seemed smaller somehow, and she couldn't seem to keep her composure. The small space only served to amplify the intoxicating, decidedly masculine scent of his cologne. The smell flooded her senses, making her feel wanton, reckless.

She did her best to pay attention to his words as he told her about his designs, but she found her mind wandering to other things. She wanted to be with this man in a way she never had before. Back when they'd dated, she was too young, and he, too respectful, to take their relationship to the ultimate physical level. She sensed that he still saw her as the young teen she used to be, and in a way, that was sweet. However, the woman in her wanted his touch, his kiss and everything that a man and a woman could share.

In an attempt to shake off those thoughts, she directed her attention back to the passing scenery.

He navigated the car along Mission Boulevard, then veered right onto La Jolla Boulevard. They rode along in silence for several miles, passing through the Bird Rock and Lower Hermosa neighborhoods, until he stopped at a construction site a short distance away from Windansea Beach.

"Where are we?" She peered out into the darkness, lit only by the neighborhood streetlights.

"This is where the museum I'm designing is going to be built."

"Wow." She looked at the cleared land, or at

least what she could see of it. "I never would have imagined a museum going up here."

"The zoning in this area is pretty flexible," he commented. "Plus, the neighborhood association didn't put up a fight once they learned about the museum, how it will be built and what it will stand for."

She nodded her understanding. "I'm impressed, Chris. You've done really well for yourself." She turned his way. "I'm proud of you."

"Thanks." He reached out, squeezed her hand. "You know, you've accomplished plenty as well."

She waved him off. "Nah. I'm just a girl chasing her passion."

"Come on. You're not giving yourself enough credit. From what I can tell, Ellicott's is already very successful. That's not an easy feat to pull off, for a business in Gaslamp that's been open less than six months."

She could see what he meant. Gaslamp was a bustling, culturally exciting area of town. The atmosphere was what had drawn her to open Ellicott's there. Still, businesses located there faced something of an uphill battle to establish themselves. An ever-changing clientele with wildly varying tastes flowed through the district, making profitability for small business owners a challenge. "I hadn't really thought of that, but I guess you're right."

"Of course I'm right." He winked. "Don't be so modest. You've done something impressive and worthy of praise."

She smiled then, feeling her cheeks warm in response to his flattery. "Thank you, Chris."

"Just calling it as I see it, and you're welcome."

Silence fell in the car for a few moments. Their gazes connected.

Eliza could feel desire rolling through her like a wave. She leaned in for his kiss, and he met her halfway. Her eyes closed as his lips touched hers. She laid her open palm against his jawline, tilting her head to the side and letting the tip of her tongue stroke his bottom lip. The gesture was meant to alert him that she wanted to be kissed fully, with passion.

Instead, he stiffened and pulled away, bringing the moment to an abrupt end.

Eliza's eyes popped open in time to see him shift the car out of Park. She straightened in her seat as he pulled away from the curb and back onto the road. "Chris? Is something wrong?"

He shook his head, keeping his straight ahead. "No, nothing's wrong. But I think I've kept you out late enough."

She rolled her eyes. "Are you kidding? I'm an adult. I don't have a curfew."

"I know. But we both have to work tomorrow, Eliza."

That statement made her ire rise. He may as well have admonished her for being out late on a school night. She inhaled deeply, then blew the breath out, but didn't say anything else. What else was there to say, when Chris was so obviously stuck in the habit of seeing her as a girl of nineteen instead of the grown woman she was?

They rode the rest of the way in silence, and when he pulled up to the cottage, she unhooked her seat belt, swung open the door and hopped out.

He must have sensed her annoyance, because unlike the last time, he didn't get out and try to follow her. And as she closed her front door and locked herself inside her house, she was glad he hadn't.

## Chapter 10

Friday afternoon, Chris leaned over his drafting table, sketching in some of the details on the floor plans for the museum. He erased a part of the line he'd just drawn, blew away the eraser dust and redrew it with the help of his straightedge. Satisfied with that section, he moved to the adjacent section to work on details there.

His phone buzzed in the pocket of his slacks, and he set down the pencil and checked the screen. It was a text message from Sheila.

Working late, please pick up Jojo from piano lesson

He fired off a quick reply, letting Sheila know he would do as she asked. A glance at the clock above his drafting table showed him the time, three forty. Since Jojo's piano lesson ended in less than an hour, he decided to pack it in for the day. He spent a few minutes straightening up, putting his tools away in the drawers beneath his drafting table.

Grabbing a bottle of water from the kitchen, he then got into his car and drove to the Young Musicians' Academy. The small school, located in the Pacific Beach neighborhood, offered private lessons in piano, violin, cello and upright bass. He pulled into an empty space in the small parking lot, let the windows down and cut the engine. He'd arrived a few minutes early, so he scrolled through the highlights on a financial news website he followed to pass the time.

Jojo strolled out, wearing a pair of dark denim jeans, sneakers and a solid blue T-shirt emblazoned with a glittery silver star. When she saw the car, she waved.

He waved back, then got out and opened the passenger-side door for her. Once he made sure she was buckled in, he closed her inside.

As he pulled out of the parking space, she asked, "Where's Mom?"

"She had to work late, so she texted me and asked me to pick you up." He rolled up the windows so they could hear each other better. "You can hang with me until she gets off."

"Can't I just go home?"

"Alone?" He scoffed. "I don't think so, young lady."

"Jack's not there?"

He shook his head. "No, he's at Carter's house, playing video games. Spoke to him earlier."

Jojo sighed. "Okay, whatever."

Keeping his focus on the road, Chris shook his head. Logically, he knew Jojo's newfound attitude had everything to do with her changing hormones and her desire to be seen as an adult. Knowing that didn't make it any easier to accept, though. He thought back to the dance last weekend, and the young man she'd danced with. "I didn't get a chance to ask you before, but what can you tell me about Anthony?"

She looked at him, eyes wide. "What?"

"You know, Anthony. The young man from the dance. Jack says you have a crush on him, so I thought I'd…"

Jojo pursed her lips. "Jack dimed me out? I'll be sure to thank him with a fat lip."

He chuckled. "Go easy on your brother. Anyway, what can you tell me about him?"

She folded her arms over her chest. "Dad, I don't really want to do this."

"Come on, Jojo. Just tell me a little bit about him." He wanted to get as much information out of her as he could while they were in the car, because he knew she'd disappear into her room once they got into the house.

"Like what?"

"Like, why do you like him? Do you two have any shared interests?"

She shrugged. "He likes some of the same music as me. And he says his mom wants him to take piano."

Chris nodded, turning off the road and into the entrance to his property. As the car moved up the steep drive, he said, "How does he treat you? Is he respectful?"

She rolled her eyes. "Yes, Dad."

"Have you kissed him?"

"Dad!" Her eyes widened, and she looked away, as if embarrassed.

"I'm sorry if this is awkward for you, Jojo, but I have to know what's on this boy's mind. You know you're not allowed to be alone with boys, right?"

She released a deep, dramatic sigh. "Yes, Dad. I know, I know."

"Just checking. And if things seem to be moving too fast between you, I want you to let me know right away."

She nodded.

"I mean it. If he ever does anything that makes you feel uncomfortable, or looks at you a certain way, or…"

"Don't worry, Dad. He doesn't look at me the way you look at Miss Eliza or anything."

Pulling into his underground garage, Chris cut the engine and looked at his daughter. He was amazed at the smooth way she'd turned the conversation around and placed the focus on him. *She's got a little of her mother in her, I see.* "Really, Jojo?"

"It's like I said, Dad. It's so obvious you like her."

He sighed, but knew their conversation about her crush was effectively over. "Come on, Jojo. Let's go inside and grab a snack."

She chuckled. "Yeah, okay, Dad."

He thought back to the way Eliza had come on to him, and how caught off guard he'd been. She'd always seemed so innocent to him, but her behavior in his car had indicated otherwise. How was he supposed to respond when Eliza's gesture had seemed to come out of nowhere?

He shook off the thought and walked with Jojo to the door leading from the garage into the den, unlocking it. Then he followed his wily daughter inside and shut the door.

Friday night found Eliza sitting on the wrap-around porch at her sister Brianne's house. The house sat in a cul-de-sac in a quiet section of the La Jolla district. It was after nine, and Eliza assumed most of the children in the neighborhood were in bed for the evening. Brianne's three daughters had been in bed for more than an hour, and her husband, Ed, had gone upstairs to catch up on his recorded television shows from the last week.

As she looked around, Eliza could see that there were more than a few people sitting out on their porches or patios, enjoying adult conversation and a glass of wine in the warm evening breeze.

Brianne, stretched out on the padded cushion of her brown wicker love seat, sighed. "So, Eliza. Tell me what's going on. We can talk now that the kids are in bed."

Sitting across from her in the matching wicker armchair, Eliza crossed her legs at the ankle. "The store was slammed today. We sold out of those new jeweled sandals with the T-strap in every color we had, and…"

Brianne raised her hand, palm out. "Girl, stop! There you go again, telling me about work as if you have no social life."

She shrugged. "I don't have much of one. It's Friday night and I'm hanging out with you." She winked.

Rolling her eyes, Brianne said, "Eliza. Don't make me pop you. What's going on with you and Chris?"

"Chris who?" She pulled the same card that Brianne had earlier in the week. "I know at least four dudes named Chris."

Her expression changed. Lips pursed in annoyance, Brianne said, "Chris Marland. Stop playing."

She giggled. "I guess I've teased you enough. But the truth, I don't have anything exciting to tell you."

Her brow arched in surprise. "Seriously? Nothing?"

Eliza shrugged. "We've kissed a few times, but that's it."

"How many times have you been out?"

She thought for a minute. "Five. And we've had a great time, every time."

"I don't get it." Brianne slumped back against the cushion.

"Believe me, I'm just as disappointed as you are." Thinking of what was happening, or not happening, between her and Chris made Eliza feel just as deflated as her sister appeared. "And it's not from lack of attraction between us."

"Obviously. You two were joined at the hip back in the day. Inseparable." Brianne seemed to be looking past her, out into the night. "We all thought you two would end up together; me, Emily, even Mom."

"So did I." She sighed. "Anyway, fate has given us a second chance, but so far it seems like some big cosmic joke. I mean, I want this man in every way a woman can want a man. But he just doesn't seem to get it."

"Do you think maybe you're being too subtle?"

"I don't know. I don't think so." She ran a hand through her hair. "There's only so much I can do out in public without coming off in the wrong way, know what I mean?"

"Yeah, I get it." Brianne rested her chin on her fingers. "Give me an example of something you've tried, maybe I can help."

Now Eliza raised her brow. "Isn't this more Emily's wheelhouse? I mean, she is the oldest, and she's a marriage counselor."

"It probably is, but she's out of town at that therapists' convention for the next week, remember?" Brianne smiled. "So just let the middle sister try to help you out, okay?"

She chuckled. "I'm willing to give it a shot. Okay, so the other night. We rode around town, looking at the buildings he'd designed. I got the impression that he was trying to impress me, and it's working."

"It does sound like he was trying to impress you."

"So, we're sitting at the site where the museum he's designing now is going to be built. It's deserted, it's dark. We're talking, and the mood is right, so I lean in for a kiss—"

"Oh, girl. He didn't kiss you?"

Eliza rolled her eyes. "Brianne, chill. We did kiss, but when I tried to slip some tongue in there, he froze up. Then he just jerked away and took me home with some line about how he'd kept me out too late."

"Damn." Brianne's eyes widened. "Y'all both grown, and he hit you with the curfew defense?"

"Yeah." Eliza cringed at the memory. "That was incredibly awkward, and frustrating."

"Now I see what you meant when you said he sees you as a teenager."

"Good. Now tell me how to break him out of that mind-set." She leaned forward in her seat. "Listen, I can appreciate him being a gentleman, because that's rare in this day and age. But I'm not a kid anymore. I'm a grown woman, with grown-woman needs, and he's got what I need."

Brianne smiled. "Well, all right, then."

"You know we never went all the way back then, right?"

Brianne nodded. "Girl, I know. None of us could get any while we were under our parents' roof. Dad did everything but make us wear chastity belts."

"Well, the time has come for me to take it there with Chris. So help me out here. What am I doing wrong?"

She was silent for a few moments, tapping her index finger on her chin. "Okay. It sounds like you've been pretty subtle up until now, which I get. I understand you not wanting to look over-zealous in public and all that. But maybe it's time to change your approach."

"How so?" At this point, Eliza was open to suggestions, because she felt like things weren't really progressing between her and Chris.

"Has Chris changed much since the old days? In terms of his attitude and personality?"

She shook her head. "No. I'd say he's more mature, but he's essentially the same guy."

"In that case, think about the kind of guy he is. He's super serious, focused, driven. You could even call him intense."

Eliza chuckled, shaking her head as she thought of his expressions and gesticulations when he spoke about his work or his kids. "*Intense* is a good word."

"Then you need to stop being subtle. This man doesn't have a subtle bone in his body, so he's not gonna respond to hints. Be obvious, be overt. Give him the full-on seduction treatment."

Eliza swallowed. "I mean, I don't know if I can pull that off. He knows I'm back in the cottage on our parents' property, and he won't set foot in there."

"So go to his place."

The lightbulb snapped on inside her head. "Marland Manor. His fortress in the hills."

"That's right. Everybody around here knows about that place. It's one of the most state-of-the-art structures on the West Coast. Just text him, tell him you want to tour his most personal creation and get the address."

She clapped her hands together. "He's not gonna turn me down. He loves showing off his work." It was the perfect plan. All she needed was an in, and she could handle the rest.

Brianne tilted her head to the side. "Go get your man, girl."

Eliza stood up, her mind formulating a plan. "Bet."

## Chapter 11

Chris sat at his drafting table Saturday night, poring over his latest revisions to the plans for the Museum of Sustainable Art. He'd nailed down most of the design and felt satisfied with what he'd come up with so far. But for some reason, he just couldn't settle on the right look for the sculpture gallery in the west wing. The museum's director had described her vision for the gallery in clear terms. She wanted an indoor section that displayed the smaller, more delicate sculptures, and an outdoor section for the larger, more hardy pieces. The hard part would be delivering the dichotomy she'd requested: the two sections were to seem distinct, yet still flow together in a seamless way.

With his years of experience in architecture, Chris knew of several techniques that could work to deliver on the director's request. Despite that, choosing which way to carry out her vision for the space, while staying true to the museum's guiding principle of using only sustainable material, proved to be a bigger challenge than he'd anticipated. *What materials can I use that will give the right look without being wasteful?* He tapped the eraser of his graphite pencil on the paper repeatedly, lost in thought.

He got up from his stool, moving to the desk on the adjacent wall. Opening his laptop, he swiped the screen to bring up his internet browser. He knew of a few alternatives to the traditional building materials he was accustomed to working with, but he couldn't think of any that fit the unique demands of this project. In the interest of doing his best work, he wanted to see what he could find. The responsibility for the use of proper materials fell to the contractor, not the architect. Still, he made it a point to stay as up-to-date as he could on matters like this, because the knowledge often informed his design process. He went to his search bar and typed in "green building materials," hoping he'd find something useful in the results.

Before the links finished populating, he heard the doorbell ring. Confusion knit his brow for a moment as he wondered who would be visiting him at home, especially after eight on a Saturday. Seconds later, he snapped his fingers as he recalled his text conversation with Eliza. She'd wanted to tour the house, having expressed interest in seeing his most important design. Looking down at his New Edition Home Again tour T-shirt and gray sweatpants, he wished he'd remembered her visit. *No time to change now.*

The doorbell rang again, and he pushed the thought aside as he padded barefoot out of the office, down the stairs and hallway, and into the sitting room to open his front door.

When his eyes landed on Eliza, standing in the soft yellow glow of his porch light, he felt his jaw go slack.

She wore a velour tracksuit in a deep shade of blue. The jacket, bedazzled around the bottom, was cut in such a way that the sparkling stones grazed the flat plane of her belly, just above her navel. The hood of the jacket was pulled up, obscuring her hair. But nothing could obscure the scorching-hot body encased in the shimmery, fitted fabric. The pants sat low on her hips, hugging her curves like a race car in the Monaco Grand Prix. He let his eyes rake over her frame, then back up to her face, where he found her gaze waiting.

"Hey, Chris." Her glossy lips turned up into a smile. "Did you forget about me coming over?"

He swallowed, nodded. "Sorry. Got caught up in a floor plan." He stood there in the open door, staring at her. A few days ago, when he looked at her, he could still see the grinning, ponytail-wearing, chemistry book–toting girl who'd first stolen his heart. But when he looked at her now, he didn't see a girl. He saw a woman, and a hell of a woman at that.

"Can I come in?" She blinked several times, the dark fringe of her lashes fluttering.

He stepped back so she could enter, then closed the door behind her. "Make yourself at home." He watched her strut past him, and when he caught a glimpse of her ass, swaying with each step, his groin tightened. *Damn.*

"Before we start the tour, can I see what you're working on? I mean, if you don't mind." Her voice broke into his thoughts.

"Sure. Follow me." He walked past her, leading her through the house to the office. Once they arrived in his office, he gestured to the floor plan clipped to his drafting table. "This is it. It's a sculpture gallery for the museum."

She strode ahead of him again, leaning over the table to peer at his drawing. Her posture treated him to another view of her ample round hips. He cleared his throat, but that did nothing for the dryness there. So he grabbed the bottle of water he'd left sitting on his desk and took a long draw.

"Thirsty, Chris?" She eyed him, her expression a mixture of amusement and curiosity.

He blew out a breath. "I…well…"

Before he could form a coherent answer to her question, she straightened. Her graceful, manicured fingertips captured the zipper pull on the front of the jacket. Her eyes locked with his, she tugged the zipper down, revealing a black lace bra beneath.

He gasped. "Shit."

She winked. Then she edged closer to him, entering his personal space.

"What are you doing, Eliza?"

By now, her breasts were pressed against his chest. "What we should have done a long time ago, Chris. I want you."

He flexed his fingers. Keeping chaste with her back then hadn't been easy, and he remembered the frustration well. But was this really what she wanted? "What about the tour?"

"Don't worry. You can show me everything after breakfast."

The realization of what she'd offered him hit him all at once, and his body reacted, hardness stretching the crotch of his pants. His eyes widened, and he licked his lips. "Eliza, I…"

She pressed her index finger to his lips. "I'm grown now, Chris. And I know what I want." Backing away, she carefully unclipped his drawing from the drafting table. Rolling it, she placed it on his desk before returning to the drafting table. Then she draped herself over it, her back resting against the slanted surface. "Less talking. More kissing."

He groaned low in his throat. What she'd said couldn't be any truer: she was grown, a woman in every sense of the word. A man had only so much willpower, and what he'd possessed had long since been burned away by this fiery seduction. He wasted no time joining her. As his body made contact with hers, their lips collided.

Her lips were soft, yielding. As their tongues mated, he could hear the sound and feel the vibration of her soft moans. The smell of her perfume, feminine and floral, filled his nostrils. Still kissing her, he undid her zipper, spreading the open halves of her jacket and splaying his palms over her belly. Her silken skin, warm beneath his touch, fueled his desire to take her fully. He broke the kiss, looked at her and groaned again. She'd overtaken his senses, and in that moment, he wanted nothing more than to bury himself between her shapely thighs and take her until she screamed his name.

"Are you sure, Eliza?"

She opened her eyes, and their gazes locked. Laying her hand against his cheek, she nodded. "I've never been this sure about anything."

A heartbeat later, he clasped his arms around her waist, hoisted her into his arms and carried her out of the office to his bedroom.

Eliza sighed as Chris laid her gently across his king-size bed. The thick gray bedding gave beneath her, making her feel as if she were lying on a cloud. She'd left her jacket behind in the office, and wasted no time wriggling out of her pants while still prone. She wanted him to see the black thong she'd worn, the match to her lacy bra.

When she kicked the pants aside, she heard him gasp. Her heart thudded in her chest like a Questlove drum solo. She wanted to say something cheeky, but desire had taken her voice.

She sat up, watching with appreciative eyes as he disrobed, quickly stripping off the gray sweatpants and fitted T-shirt he wore. The floor lamp near the dresser illuminated the muscled expanse of his bare torso and arms, as well as his powerful thighs.

She felt her tongue dart out across her bottom lip. Chris had the best body she'd ever seen on a man, bar none. She knew in that moment that no one else would ever be able to compete with him in her mind.

In nothing but his blue boxer briefs, he joined her on the bed. Lying on his back, he tugged her atop him until she came to rest on her knees, straddling his hips. The hard evidence of his need for her jutted up between them, stroking against her inner thigh.

She inhaled sharply, then leaned down for his kiss.

He buried his fingertips in her hair, guiding the angle of her face to his liking, and she melted like butter dropped in a hot skillet as he massaged her scalp. The way he kissed her in that moment let her know that he'd finally given up seeing her as a teenager. No, he kissed her the way a grown man kissed a grown woman, and she loved every second of it.

Passion took hold, and before she could stop herself, she began to move her hips, working her lower body against his. She'd never done anything so wanton before, but she couldn't stop. She liked the sensation of his hardness rubbing against her too much to stop. A warm, wonderful pulsation between her legs made her want to keep going. And if his grunts were any indication, he liked it as well.

He slipped his hands out of her hair, moving them to either side of her waist, and stayed her. "If you keep doing that, the show will be over before it starts."

She bit her lip, smiling. "Sorry."

"Don't apologize. Just give me a minute to grab the condom."

She shifted aside, letting him get up. He took a foil packet from the drawer of his nightstand, and as she watched, he snatched off his boxer briefs. Her eyes rounded as she saw his girth, and the throbbing between her thighs increased to a fever pitch as she watched him roll the protection on. Finished with that, he flicked off the lamp.

He came back to the bed and wasted no time kissing and caressing her out of her bra and panties. She sighed and gasped through the undressing, and when he laid her down again and climbed on top of her, she closed her eyes against the blooming passion that threatened to overwhelm her.

He kissed her lips, then her cheeks, then her eyelids, then moved down to kiss the column of her throat. "Open up for me, baby."

She parted her trembling thighs, feeling him prodding there. Soon he found her opening and slipped into her warmth. She felt her body stretching, molding to him, and by the time he began stroking her, she disintegrated into ecstasy. His body moving within her own felt as natural as her heartbeat and as blissful as the sunrise over the sea. She wrapped her arms around him and clung to him, moving in time with him. Every cell, every nerve in her body, sang for him, the glow of pleasure spreading through her like a five-alarm fire consuming dry brush.

He raised his hips, then pushed them down again, his strokes long and even. She felt the fire building in her core and heard her own moans of pleasure rising in the silence around them. She lifted her lower body off the soft bedding, letting her hips rise to meet his thrusts and loving the increased pleasure of this new angle.

His groans grew louder and his movements more intense, and she joined him, caught up in the rising passion. He moved his hands to cup her ass, his grasp firm, but gentle. She arched, and at his next stroke, she shattered, screaming his name.

He followed her to paradise moments later, still gripping her, his body shuddering with the force of his release.

She felt him leave her body as he rolled next to her. Then he gathered her into his arms, kissing the top of her hair as she drifted to sleep.

In the deep of night, Eliza startled awake from a strange dream. Blinking a few times, she felt confusion sweep over her as she glanced around the unfamiliar surroundings. That, combined with the weight of a muscular arm draped over her waist and the hard body pressed against her back, made her feel somewhat disoriented.

The feeling lasted only a few seconds as sleep wore off and reality set in. The room, quiet save for Chris's soft snores, loomed large around her. Moonlight streamed in through the sheer curtains, keeping the shadows at bay. Beyond the bedroom door lay the still-unexplored depths of his mountainside retreat. She supposed they'd get around to the tour…sometime. Right now, she was content to lie in his arms.

As memories of their lovemaking flooded her mind, she smiled. Her body still echoed with remnants of the passion they'd shared. Being with him in real life had exceeded every fantasy her mind had ever conjured, and she felt pleased that he'd finally come to see her as she was now, as opposed to who she used to be. Years ago, she'd loved him with all her heart, despite her parents' insistence that she was too young to know her own mind. Making love with him had only brought those feelings back, and it surprised her that the feelings were just as intense now as they'd been back then.

*Am I really falling for him?* Deep down, she could feel the affection he had for her. He'd always treated her with the utmost care, and tonight had been no exception. She felt certain that he loved her, but who knew if he was ready to admit it? And if he wasn't ready, where did that leave her? It was all too much to consider, especially since she was only half-awake.

She felt a tickle in her nose, and she had just enough time to grab a tissue from the box on his nightstand before she sneezed.

She crumpled the tissue and tossed it into the wastebasket. When she settled back down, she saw that Chris had awakened and was staring right at her. She rolled over to face him, offered a crooked smile. "Sorry, didn't mean to wake you."

"No worries." He pulled her body closer to his, snuggling against her.

She sighed. It was so nice to be held this way, and being with someone she felt so comfortable with made it even better.

He inhaled deeply. "Your hair smells like grapefruits."

She chuckled, amused by his quirky observation. "I use a shampoo with citrus oil."

"I like it. Keep using it."

Between them, she felt his body awakening. It was as if his body were reacting to her nearness. "Chris…"

"I know." He smiled. "How about another ride? Just not in my car this time."

She licked her lips and straddled him. "Okay. But watch your speed."

"Don't worry." He leaned up to kiss her as their bodies came together. "We'll go nice and slow."

## Chapter 12

Late Sunday morning, Chris sat in a lounger by his pool, a cup of coffee in hand. Eliza reclined on the lounger next to him, nursing her own cup.

He looked her way, admiring her beauty. She looked totally relaxed and at home, dressed in one of his old white tees and nothing else. Due to his height, the shirt's hem grazed her knees, and the expanse of her long, shapely legs was bared to his eyes.

She glanced toward him, smiled. "It's beautiful out here."

"Thanks." He'd built this place as his personal

retreat, and had poured the best of his architectural skills into the design. "The pool deck is my favorite area of the house."

"I can understand that. It's unique." She gazed out over the white marble deck toward the water. "I just have one question."

"What's that?"

"Where does the water end?"

He chuckled. He'd spent a great deal of time and effort creating just the right design for his custom one-of-a-kind home, and the curved infinity pool was the jewel of his mountain retreat. "Without getting too complicated, it's kind of like a huge fountain. Just over the edge of the deck, there's another marble step that the water runs over. Beneath that, there's a hidden reservoir and a pump system that cycles the water back into the upper level of the pool."

"Nice." She sounded impressed. "And what's on the other side of the reservoir?"

"The mountain." He laughed. "Just brush and grass. I didn't develop any of that; I picked this spot because I wanted privacy and didn't need a lawn. I wasn't interested in the upkeep."

"I get that. At any rate, this place is magical. I feel like I'm at some kind of fairy-tale palace."

"If that's true, that would make you the queen."

She blushed. "Okay, smooth talker."

He winked, then took a drink from his coffee cup. The weather, sunny and temperate, made it a perfect day for sitting out on the pool deck, and he couldn't ask for better company. "So, now that I've given you the tour, what's your favorite part of the house?" They'd spent about a half hour earlier walking through the place, and she'd taken in all the sights with great interest. Knowing she was nude beneath the borrowed shirt hadn't made it easy to concentrate on explaining the finer parts of the design to her, but he'd promised her a tour and had delivered.

She sighed, sounding content. "Actually, I think the pool deck is my favorite part. The deck and pool are pretty awesome, and then when you add in this magnificent view of the city and the mountains, it's truly special." She gestured out toward the horizon.

His brow hitched. *Yet another thing we have in common.*

"At first, I wondered why you would choose to live so far away from everyone and everything. It took a while to get here, and then trying to get up that steep driveway was a killer."

He chuckled. "I know. It weeds out the solicitors and other folks I don't want to visit me."

"I bet." She shook her head, giggling. "Anyway, now that I've come up here and seen the house and the views, I totally understand. What a wonderful place to call home."

"Since I live and work here, I aimed to make it feel like a vacation retreat; an escape from the rat race, if you will." Draining the last of his coffee, he sat his empty cup down on the glass table next to his lounger.

She was silent for a few moments as she sipped her coffee.

He thought about how they'd spent last night. Making love to her had been amazing; he'd loved the way she'd responded to his touch. Looking at her now made him want to lift the shirt and take her all over again, here in the cool mountain breeze with the sun shining down on them. But before he could do that, there was something he needed to know. "Eliza, do your parents know we're together?"

She set her cup aside and turned his way, her gaze serious. "That's an odd question. But the answer is no. I don't make it a habit to tell them about my love life—at least, not anymore."

He shifted in his seat. "And how did that change come about?"

She shrugged. "They're so overbearing and

judgmental. If I even mention a man, they start asking me a bunch of questions about him and his 'intentions.' Sometimes it goes on for months after I've broken up with a guy. So I just gave up on explaining it to them." She waved her hand in the air, as if dismissing the issue. "Besides, I'm too old to be telling them all my business."

He agreed with her statement, but he didn't know if Colonel Ellicott would ever really stop trying to protect Eliza like a hawk watching over its young. As baby of the family, Eliza had been the last to go off to college, and the Colonel had seemed to be determined to keep her living under his rule forever. As much as he respected the Colonel, Chris had seen him as something of a tyrant back in those days.

"In fact, my mom told me to lay off introducing them to guys."

That surprised him, because he remembered how much Mrs. Ellicott loved to entertain. He couldn't imagine her turning down an opportunity to show off her home. "Oh, really?"

She nodded. "Yes. Her exact words were, 'Don't bring another man home unless you mean business.'"

He chuckled. "What a demand. So, do you mean business with me?"

"Oh, yes." She stretched, raising her arms above her head. Arching her back, she lengthened her body in a very feline manner, the hem of the shirt rising ever so slightly.

He swallowed as the blood began to rush to his lower regions. "You do?"

"Mmm-hmm." She hummed her affirmative response as she stood, slowly walking toward where he sat. "I take your business very, very seriously." Her eyes locked with his for a moment before she made a show of eyeing the crotch of his basketball shorts.

He groaned as she entered his space and eased the shirt up around her waist. Then she sat on his lap, one leg on either side of the lounger.

"In fact," she said, grazing her fingertip over his jawline, "I think we should get back to business right now."

A moment ago, he'd had more questions about her parents. But now, as he dragged her down to his kiss, all thoughts of conversation fled, leaving behind only his desire to fill her until she shouted for joy.

Eliza used her key to open the back door of her parents' house and walked into the kitchen. It was midmorning, the second Tuesday in July, and the aroma of fresh-brewed coffee greeted her as she entered, closing the door behind her. She glanced around the empty kitchen, then listened for sounds that would help her locate her parents. Hearing the television playing in the parlor, she stopped at the counter to make herself a cup of coffee, then carried it with her toward the sound.

Her father, Commander Vaughn Ellicott Sr., sat on the white chintz sofa, his eyes trained on an episode of *In the Heat of the Night* playing on the big-screen television. He must have heard her footsteps on the carpet, because he turned his head in her direction as soon as she crossed the threshold.

"Reporting for daughter duty," she said, standing at attention and giving a crisp salute. She and her siblings often did that kind of thing, harkening back to their father's long and illustrious career in the US Navy. Vaughn had admired his father so much that he'd gone into the navy himself after high school.

He chuckled. "At ease. Good morning, sweetheart."

"Morning, Dad." She came over to where he sat and bent to place a kiss on his forehead. "Where's Mom? We're supposed to be going shopping."

He shrugged. "I think she's still upstairs."

Eliza smiled. It was obvious her father's focus

was on the old television show he was watching, so she left him alone. "I'm going to go up and get her, okay?"

He nodded, but didn't take his eyes off the screen.

She crossed the parlor and entered the foyer. There, on the bottom rung of the staircase, she stopped and looked at her father. For whatever reason, he seemed to be wearing his age today. The gray patches near his temples, the glasses perched on the end of his nose, and even the lines starting to show around his mouth and forehead stood out to her in a way they never had before.

She loved her father very much, but he'd been hard to please. As his baby, she'd wanted his approval more than anything. If she were honest with herself, she still craved that approval, even though she was grown. It was her longing for his approval that kept her from being honest with him about getting involved with Chris again.

It had been two and half blissful weeks since they'd made love, and she and Chris had been spending as much time together as their schedules allowed. No one in her entire family, except her sister Brianne, knew about Eliza and Chris's relationship. Eliza had sworn Brianne to secrecy, and Brianne, relishing the idea of knowing something about her sister that no one else did, had kept it to herself.

She supposed her father could have changed his opinion of Chris over the years. Maybe he'd forgiven Chris for leaving her with a broken heart back then and would embrace the idea of them reconciling. But parts of her didn't want to tell her father, because things were just starting to settle out with Chris, and she didn't want to mess that up.

With a sigh, she started up the stairs, seeking her mother. She found Natalie Ellicott seated on the end of the bed in the master suite, phone in hand.

When Eliza entered the room, Natalie looked up and spoke into the receiver. "Okay, Jean. I'll have to call you back later, my daughter's here." After disconnecting the call, she smiled her way. "Morning, Eliza. I'm just about ready. Let me get my purse and we can go."

"Okay, Mom."

Her mother disappeared into the walk-in closet, returning with her favorite black leather handbag. As she slung the strap over her shoulder, she stopped, eyeing her. "Eliza, is something wrong?"

Realizing her expression had given away her melancholy, she sought a quick cover story. The first one to pop into her head was, thankfully, a true one. "Listen, Mom. I've been thinking about moving out of the cottage." She'd been thinking about it ever since she'd closed out her first day at five-figure sales in the boutique. While she loved her parents, she craved the full measure of privacy she could enjoy as an adult. And while the cottage was about a half mile from the main house, she was still essentially a boarder on her parents' property.

Natalie frowned, showing her disappointment. "Oh, really? You know there's no rush for you to leave, dear. We love having you so close to home, especially after you spent all that time living on the other side of the country."

She recalled how often her parents had spoken of missing her when she'd been living in New York, running her boutique there. Closing her shop, then packing up her life and moving back home after her breakup with Burton, had been quite an undertaking, but now she was glad she'd made the journey. "I know, and it's been great. But I really think it's time I start looking for a place. Somewhere in the city, maybe. Closer to the boutique."

They left the bedroom, went down the stairs together. On the first floor, Natalie took a moment to give Vaughn Sr. a quick kiss before they both exited through the kitchen door.

As they climbed into Eliza's sedan, Natalie remarked, "When you came home, you said you wanted to use the cottage until you felt the store was well established. Do you feel that it is? It's only been a few months."

Eliza started the car, pulling away from the house. "Yes, Mom. I really do. Business is brisk at the boutique, and I've saved up some money. I'm thinking I may have enough to put down on a nice condominium or apartment." Her more idealistic self often fantasized about moving into Marland Manor with Chris, but she had better sense than to mention that fantasy to her mother.

"All right, dear. If it's what you really want, you know I won't stand in your way." Natalie clasped her purse in her lap, the way she always did when riding in a car. "I can't speak for your father, though."

Eliza sighed. She knew her father wouldn't be thrilled to hear of her moving out of the cottage and moving on with her life, but she couldn't let that stop her from doing what felt right. And that applied both to getting her own place and to being with the man she'd fallen in love with all over again.

# Chapter 13

Wednesday afternoon, Chris reclined in his lounger on the pool deck, enjoying the view of the mountains. He'd turned in his final plans for the Museum of Sustainable Art earlier, and had decided to take the rest of the day off in celebration. For now, his only company was an ice-cold beer, but he was expecting Eliza to come over later and help him celebrate fully.

A smile tilted his lips as he thought of all the ways he wanted to touch her. The past few weeks had been great; having her back in his life seemed to make everything better.

The ringing of his cell phone caught his attention. Setting down the beer bottle, he grabbed the phone from his pocket and looked at the screen. His eyes widened when he saw who was calling. He took a deep breath and answered the call. "Dr. Clark. How are you?"

"Good afternoon, Mr. Marland." As assistant national director of the Prescott George organization, Dr. Clark was known for being a straight shooter. "Forgive me if I skip the pleasantries, but what is going on in the San Diego chapter these days?"

"Well, sir, we're working on a community service project now. We're going to fund a building and the operation of a youth center in a low-income area and of course we're continuing our program of purchasing backpacks and school supplies and…"

"Nice try. You know that's not what I'm referring to, Chris."

"I'm not exactly sure what you're asking me, sir."

Dr. Clark sighed. "Chris, we keep up with the activities of every chapter of Prescott George. We've seen the negative press the San Diego chapter has been getting. We've read about the break-in, the vandalism and the mismanagement of funds, and this doesn't present our organization in the best light. Just what kind of dog and pony show are you running out there?"

Chris sighed. "Dr. Clark, the chapter leadership is looking into these matters. We haven't gotten to the bottom of them yet, but we're confident we will soon."

"You'd better. Because if you don't straighten all this out, we may have to cancel the gala."

Chris bolted upright in his seat. "Dr. Clark, you can't be serious. That gala is six days away."

"I'm very serious. I never joke about things like this."

He cringed. "Surely there must be some way for us to work this out. Think of the expense the organization has gone to for the party. Canceling it now would lead to a serious loss of funds."

"I know that. But if you don't deal with the PR issue at your chapter, the Chapter of the *Year*, the repercussions could be even worse. You have three business days, Chris. Either fix this or expect us to cancel the party." That said, Dr. Clark disconnected the call.

Stunned, Chris tucked his phone back into his pocket. He grabbed his beer, slumped against the lounger and drained the rest of the bottle. This mess at Prescott George had been the bane of his existence for the past few months, and now things were about to come to a head. He'd been so excited to discover that his chapter had been chosen Chapter of the Year. It was a recognition of the work he and his chapter mates had done, both in their professional fields and in their community. Now, with the possible loss of that honor hanging over his head, he didn't know how to fix things. Frustration coursed through him, making him feel restless. He knew that whenever he felt this way, the only way to break out of it was physical activity. Getting up from the lounger, he went inside the house to change and returned a few minutes later in a pair of black swim trunks.

He went to the edge of the pool deck and stared down into the blue water. The pool had a single depth, eight feet. He loved to swim, and found it relaxed him in a way that other workouts couldn't match. Lifting his arms, he dived in, breaking the surface with a splash.

Under the water, he swam laps along the curved length of the pool, staying to the upper section away from the waterfall. As he cut through the water, he felt the tension melting away with each stroke of his arms. His mind cleared, allowing him to think reasonably about the situation without involving his personal feelings. As his arms started to burn from exertion, he swam back to the edge of the pool and lifted himself out of the water.

He was drying his face with a thick white towel when he heard footsteps. Tossing the towel aside, he looked in the direction of the sound and saw Eliza walking toward him. She wore a soft pink sundress and flat sandals. The top of the dress bared her shoulders, and the hem grazed her midthigh, revealing the length of her gorgeous legs. Her hair hung loose, flowing in the breeze around her face like a wavy brown halo.

"I thought you'd be out here." She smiled as she entered his space. "Congrats on finishing your design, honey."

"Thank you." Seeing her put him right back in the celebratory mood. He kissed her on the cheek, wrapped his arms around her and drew her close. She smelled of flowers and citrus. His body immediately reacted to her presence, and in the thin swimming trunks there was no way to hide it.

She must have felt it, because she looked down and then back up again. "I love that you're so happy to see me."

"You look amazing." He let his greedy eyes run over her frame again.

"Thank you. I'm glad you like it."

"I love it." He saw the drops of water staining

the dress. "Sorry, I just got out of the pool. I should have dried off before I got you all wet." It was out of his mouth before he realized how it sounded.

Her expression changed then, her sweet smile morphing into something wicked. "Don't worry about it. You getting me all wet is part of why I'm here."

He licked his lips. "Then what the hell are we standing here for?"

She laughed, and after he opened the pool deck door, she slipped inside. He followed her and shut the door behind them.

When they reached the stairs, she went up first. He lingered a few seconds behind her, watching as the hem of the dress rose in time with her steps, revealing the tempting curve of her ass. He knew then that they weren't going to make it upstairs.

She gasped as he lips brushed against the back of her thigh. "Chris, what are you…" Her words melted into moans as he continued, kissing and licking her there. Stopping, she gripped the handrail and leaned on it for support.

He helped her sit, then eased the dress up around her waist and caressed her out of her panties. As she lay back on the stairs, he parted her thighs and knelt a few steps below her. Then he leaned forward placed his kisses there until she cried out.

He left her then, sneaking away while she rode out her orgasm, returning naked and wearing a condom. She opened her eyes, leaned up for his kiss. He kissed her lips, letting his tongue mate with hers. When he pulled away, she mewled a protest, but quieted as he gently helped her to stand and turned her toward the railing. He came behind her then, slipping inside her tight warmth, and took her until she screamed his name.

Later, he reclined in the garden tub in his master bathroom with her in his lap. He didn't know which felt better; the steaming hot water surrounding them or the womanly curves pressed against him.

"You've been quiet. Something on your mind?"

He looked down at her, snuggled against him with her head resting on his chest. Looking into her eyes, he knew it was safe to tell her what was bothering him. He trusted her and felt comfortable enough with her to reveal his thoughts. So he told her about the issues at Prescott George and the looming threat of the gala being canceled.

When he was done, she placed a soft kiss against his lips. "Thanks for being open with me, Chris. I'm really sorry things are so stressful right now."

He gave her a squeeze. "Just having you in my arms helps a lot."

She smiled. "You're a responsible person, so I know you've taken action to fix the situation."

He nodded. "I have. We even hired a private detective, but we're still waiting on his report."

"Then try not to worry so much, honey. If you've done all you can, you just have to trust that things will work out."

He looked at her then and remembered similar conversations they'd had when they were younger. She'd always believed in him, and at a time like this, her faith mattered more than ever.

And if she believed he could handle things, then damn it, he'd find a way.

# Chapter 14

When Chris arrived at the Prescott George office Thursday morning, he found Vaughn waiting at the table in the main area. Robert Yates, the private detective they'd hired, sat to Vaughn's right. Setting down his briefcase on the floor, Chris eased into the seat to Vaughn's right, at the head of the table.

After they exchanged greetings, Chris asked, "What do you have for us, Mr. Yates?"

"I've got a full report on the vandalism incident at Mr. Jace's gallery." Producing a thick stack of paper, he handed it to Chris. "I've found another piece of evidence that I think will remove any doubt of who is responsible."

"Have you seen this, Vaughn?" Chris asked.

Vaughn nodded, but remained stoic and silent.

Chris's brow furrowed as he noted Vaughn's manner. He looked down at the pages in his hand, skimming through the typewritten text. When he saw his daughter's name there, his eyes widened. "Again with this? Why does Jojo's name keep coming up?"

Vaughn sighed. "I'm guessing you didn't read very far, man."

Chris turned questioning eyes to Robert. "What's going on?"

Robert shifted in his seat, but answered the question anyway. "As you know, last month your daughter's bracelet was found under a table in Jordan Jace's studio the night his sculpture was vandalized. Now, the new evidence is an eyewitness who was at the party at the gallery the night the vandalism occurred. She claims she saw your daughter go into Jace's studio right before the vandalism occurred—and she saw Jojo put her hands on the statue. At first she didn't think anything of it, just a teenager admiring a sculpture in progress. But when news of the vandalism came out, she offered a signed statement—it's in the packet of paperwork I just handed you."

Shaking his head, Chris tossed down the papers and rested his forehead in his hand. "I can't believe my little girl would do something like this."

Robert offered, "it would be helpful if you could get her here."

"She and Jack are attending a summer arts program not too far from here." Chris sighed. "Let me call her."

Chris stepped away from the table to make the call. About twenty minutes later, he was back in his seat when Jojo entered the office.

She glanced around at all the faces at the table. "Hi, Dad. What's going on?"

"Have a seat, Jojo."

She did as he asked, sitting down across from Vaughn and next to her father. "Hi, Mr. Ellicott."

Vaughn offered a slight smile. "Hi, Jojo."

"Go ahead, Mr. Yates." Chris kept his eyes on his daughter while Robert explained his findings.

"So based on this evidence, Ms. Marland, I believe you were responsible for the vandalism of Mr. Jace's sculpture." Robert clasped his hands on the tabletop.

Chris noticed the fear and guilt in his daughter's eyes, and in that moment, he knew it was true. Tears filled her eyes. Grappling with his disappointment over his daughter's actions, he said, "Jojo? What do you have to say for yourself?"

The tears spilling down her cheeks, Jojo nodded. "Yes, Daddy. I did it. I'm the one who wrecked Mr. Jace's sculpture."

Chris touched her shoulder. "Jojo, I'm surprised at you. How could you do this?"

"I did it because I was mad!" She all but shouted the words between her sobs. "You love this stupid club more than you love me! Yeah, lately you've been spending more time with me, but that's new. I'm sorry, Dad. I shouldn't have done it. I'm really sorry." She got up and bolted from the room. A few moments later, they heard the door to the restroom slam.

Chris sat back in his chair, releasing a long sigh. He'd have a long talk with Jojo later. "Thank you for the report, Mr. Yates. What do we need to do next?" He slipped the papers into his briefcase.

"Well, Mr. Marland, these are serious offenses. We're talking breaking and entering, plus supplying false information to the newspapers…"

"I don't know anything about that."

The men all turned to see Jojo standing in the hallway, a wad of crumpled tissue in her hand.

Mr. Yates asked, "Have you ever spoken to any reporter or journalist about Prescott George?"

She shook her head. "I never talk to anyone about Daddy's club. Why would I do that?"

The men exchanged looks.

Vaughn spoke up first. "Obviously something else is at play here. Jojo admitted what she did at the gallery. And I believe her when she says she didn't break into Prescott George or speak to the press."

Robert nodded. "I agree."

Jojo sniffled. "Thanks, Mr. Ellicott."

"We need to make a list of potential enemies of the chapter," Robert suggested.

Chris took clean paper and a pen from his briefcase, and the three of them discussed a few names.

"What about Sheila?" Vaughn brought up her name. "You're seeing someone, aren't you?"

Chris frowned. "I don't know. I mean, I wouldn't put it past her, but these problems started months ago, before I got involved with Eliza."

Vaughn tensed. "You're seeing my sister again?"

Chris shrugged. "Yeah, man. I thought you knew?"

"I didn't," Vaughn said tersely.

"That's unimportant right now." Chris tapped the tip of his pen on the table. "I guess I can try to find out if Sheila was involved. I've gotta talk to her about Jojo anyway." He wasn't looking forward to what he knew would be an unpleasant conversation with his ex-wife, but as Jojo's mother, she needed to be made aware of the situation.

"We can reconvene tomorrow, if you like." Robert looked toward Chris.

"Sure. I'll give you a call." Chris stood and grabbed his briefcase. "Right now, I need to take Jojo home. Vaughn, is there anything pressing going on here today?"

Vaughn shook his head. "Nothing I can't handle."

"Okay. Let's go, Jojo." Taking his daughter by the hand, Chris led her out.

He could feel Vaughn's eyes on his back as he exited, but he didn't turn around or look back.

Eliza lay across her bed that evening with an open a book in front of her. She'd been trying to finish the book for weeks now, and her busy schedule made that a difficult task. Now she'd finally reached the last chapter, and as she flipped the page, she couldn't wait to see how the story would end.

The ringing of her cell phone broke the silence just as she turned the second-to-last page. Annoyed, she swept it up from the nightstand and answered it. "Hello?"

"When were you going to tell me you're seeing Chris again?"

She frowned. "Well, hello to you, too, Vaughn."

"Yeah, yeah. We can skip all that, just answer my question."

She couldn't help rolling her eyes. "I don't have to tell you everything I do. I'm grown, or have you forgotten?"

He scoffed. "If you're so grown up, why are you sneaking around with him like some hormonal coed?"

"You're taking this a little too far, bro."

"Am I? I don't know why you would go out with him again, not after the way he abandoned you."

She stiffened. Her brother had purposely touched on a sore spot, and she resented his tactic. "That was a long time ago. We've both grown since then."

"How can you be so sure?"

Her lips tightened. "Vaughn, I'm not going to have this conversation with you. I don't owe you any explanations for how I live my life, and you'd do well to remember that. Because the next time you call me, questioning me about my private life,

I'm gonna forget you're my brother and go upside your head!"

"Eliza, I…"

She didn't hear the rest of his statement because she hung up on him. The nerve of him, calling her and trying to shout her down as if she were a child being scolded for doing something wrong. Setting her phone to silent, she tossed it aside and went back to reading her book.

A few minutes later, after the ending of the book put her back in a good mood, she got up and went to her kitchen to grab a snack. She was halfway up the stairs with a bag of microwave popcorn and a bottle of water when she heard her doorbell ring. Confusion knit her brow as she wondered who would stop by tonight. *If it's Vaughn, I swear I'll box his ears.*

She turned around and descended the stairs, leaving her snack on the coffee table as she passed, and went to the front door. Standing on her tiptoes, she checked the peephole. A smile stretched her lips when she saw who was there, and she unlocked the door and opened it. "Hi, Chris. What are you doing here?"

He looked utterly delicious in a black polo shirt and a pair of dark denim jeans, but his expression was serious. "Hi, baby. I really needed to talk to you. Is this a good time?"

She looked down at her pajama-clad body, wishing she'd chosen a silky gown over this cotton camisole and shorts. She stepped back to allow him inside. "Come on in."

He entered the living room, took a seat on the sofa. She sat to his right, and he put his arm around her shoulder. "It's been a hell of a crazy day. I had to tell you all the things that happened today."

She appreciated his willingness to open up to her. "I'd love to hear it, but you know, you didn't have to come all the way over here. You could have just called me."

"Nah. I didn't mind the drive. You've driven up the side of my mountain plenty." He gave her a squeeze. "Plus, I couldn't hold you over the phone, could I?"

She smiled, shook her head. "I guess not. So, what do you want to talk about?"

He drew a deep breath. "The detective we hired to look into Prescott George's problems gave his report today. We still don't know who's behind the break-in at our office and leaking those negative headlines to the newspapers, but we sat down and worked up a list of people who might be enemies of the chapter."

"I know you were hoping for more, but give it time. I'm sure things will settle out." She scratched her chin. "Wasn't there some other incident? Something about an art gallery?"

"Yeah. Jordan Jace, a Prescott George member, had one of his sculptures damaged, and he accused my daughter of doing it."

Her eyes widened. "What did you say to him?"

"I told him he was full of crap. But now that the report is in, it looks like Jojo did vandalize Jordan's sculpture after all." He looked wounded, as if just saying those words hurt him.

"Oh, no." She touched his shoulder. "I'm sorry. I know this can't be easy."

"It isn't. I just had a rather unpleasant discussion with Sheila, telling her what happened and trying to decide on the right consequences. It's not just about punishing Jojo, it's about making her think about what she did and discouraging her from ever doing anything like this again."

"Wow." She thought about that and how it must be only one of many factors that went into parenting decisions.

"And it's not just that. Jordan decided not to press charges against Jojo, but I'm going to have to eat about a ton of crow the next time I see him."

His discomfort was so palpable, she grimaced.

"That sounds unpleasant. Did Jojo give you any insight into why she would do something like this? It just doesn't seem like her."

"It's not like her. That's why I was so angry at Jordan for accusing her." He ran a hand over his forehead. "But when I heard her reasoning today, it just crushed me." He paused.

She watched him, not wanting to press but eager to hear what had motivated Jojo to pull such a stunt.

"She said she was mad because I care more about Prescott George than I care about her."

She sucked in a breath. "Ouch."

"You're telling me. I felt like a terrible father when I heard her say that."

"Goodness." She shook her head. "I feel really terrible for both of you. This is rough. And as far as Jojo, I don't condone what she did, but I suppose I understand, to a degree."

His eyes narrowed. "What do you mean by that?"

She shrugged. Wasn't it obvious to him? "What she did was wrong, but I understand her frustration. I know what it's like to feel abandoned by someone you love."

He fell silent then, studying her face. After a

few long moments, he asked, "Is that how you felt when I left all those years ago?"

She nodded, unsure of how to put her emotions into words as the memory of that old pain rose within her.

"Oh, my God. I never realized…" He clasped both of her hands within his own. "I'm sorry, Eliza. I never meant to cause you pain."

She felt a tear ease down her cheek, dashed it away. "No biggie. What's done is done, right?"

He squeezed her hands. "I can't change what I did in the past, but please know that I'm sorry. Seeing you cry really makes me think about how things went down. Maybe I should have stood up to your parents, but it seemed like they had your best interests in mind."

She frowned, confused. "What?"

"Your parents. I was trying to respect their wishes and your dreams."

That only confused her more. "Chris, I don't know what you're talking about. What do my parents have to do with any of this?"

"Your mom and dad pointed out how young you were, and how you had your whole life ahead of you. They didn't want me holding you back from a bright future. I've often thought that if we stayed together then, we might not have accomplished all the things we have in our lives."

Her heart thudded in her chest. "Are you saying my parents asked you to walk out on me?"

He released her hands, putting his own hands up defensively. "I didn't say that."

She narrowed her eyes. "Chris. Tell me."

## Chapter 15

Chris eased away from her, sensing her growing anger. He didn't think it was a good idea to go on with this conversation, because it would only lead to trouble. Her manner and her line of questioning told him she had no knowledge about the true reason their relationship had ended, and he didn't think she wanted to hear it now.

She fixed him with a hard stare. "I'm waiting, Chris."

He tried to de-escalate the conversation, hoping he could move it to more pleasant topics. "Eliza, it's water under the bridge. I don't think…"

"Tell me!" She all but shouted the words.

He sighed, realizing she wouldn't relent in her insistence on knowing the truth. "Your dad told me I had two choices. I could walk away from you, or he would see to it that my architecture career never got off the ground."

She blinked several times. "You're not serious."

He nodded. "I am. The Colonel was very clear that he thought I was a distraction to you, and that I needed to get out of your life, or he'd make mine a living hell. I couldn't afford to have my career quashed before I even got it off the ground."

She fell silent, her lips tight.

"He knows so many people in high positions, Eliza. Executives, government officials, captains of industry. I knew if I didn't do what he said, he'd make good on his threat. Think about it, Eliza. Have you ever known the Colonel to renege on his word?"

She snorted a dry, bitter laugh. "No. I sure haven't."

"Then you understand why I..."

She cut him off, scooting away from him and climbing to her feet. "Oh, I understand perfectly. I understand that you and my parents got together and planned my life for me. That you three decided what would be best for me without any input from me." Her beautiful face twisted into a mixture of fury and heartbreak.

His felt his heart squeeze inside his chest as he watched the tears sliding down her cheeks. "Eliza, please."

"Please what, Chris?" She started pacing the floor. "I don't know who I'm angrier with, you, for not standing up to my dad, or my parents for doing this mess." She stopped pacing for a moment, looking at him pointedly. "And why am I just hearing this now? Why didn't you tell me back then why you were leaving?"

"What difference would it have made?" He got up, walked over to where she stood in the center of the living room. "You needed your family. You needed to finish school and make your dreams come true. What you didn't need was an older man getting in the way of all that."

Her eyes turned cold then.

He reached out to touch her, and she dodged him.

Tears still standing in her eyes, she said in a low, incredulous voice, "That wasn't your decision to make, Chris."

He backed off, sensing she needed space.

"I think you should go."

"Eliza. Baby, please, let me try to explain." He

tried to look into her eyes, but saw only a fleeting glimpse of her turmoil before she turned her back to him.

"I don't want to hear it, Chris." She didn't even bother to turn around. "I need time to think."

"Baby..."

"Just. Get. Out."

Seeing the tense set of her shoulders, he sighed. It didn't matter what he had to say, she wasn't going to receive any of it. Knowing there wasn't anything else he could say or do, he went to the door and opened it. "Eliza," he said quietly. "I love you."

She didn't respond.

A few silent moments later, he walked out of the cottage, closing the door behind him.

He'd taken two steps when he heard the door latch behind him, followed by the muffled sounds of her sobs.

Feeling like a total jackass, he trudged to his car.

Saturday night, an exhausted Eliza made her last rounds of the store. She would close within the hour, and the weekend crowd of Ellicott's shoppers had thinned to a trickle. While she normally hated it when there was a slump in business, she didn't mind now. The store had been jumping all day, and she'd been on her feet for five straight hours. Her tired feet and aching back begged for a break from all the work she'd put in.

She'd spent half of Thursday night sobbing into a wad of tissues. One of the greatest heartaches of her life had been caused by her parents' meddling and Chris's going along with their wishes. All these years, she'd been wondering what she said, what she did, that had made Chris break things off with her the way he had. Now, to find out it hadn't even been about her but about what her father wanted for her filled her with a mixture of anger and sadness. Her right to make a major decision in her life had been taken away from her by the people she loved most. They'd stolen her autonomy, choosing to treat her like a child instead of a capable, reasonable adult. Discovering the way they'd dismissed her feelings and opinions had left her devastated and humiliated.

Friday morning, after she awakened, she'd washed her tear-streaked face, revived her puffy eyes and headed to the store. Other than the twelve hours the store had been closed since then, she'd been in the boutique ever since. It wasn't like her to work this hard on the weekend, and truthfully, she didn't need to. She had a manager she trusted to handle things, and a competent staff. The great people working for her enabled her to spend her weekends any way she wanted, and usually, she'd have been at the harbor soaking up the sunshine, or at home curled up with a good book.

This weekend was different, though, and she knew why. She had both a broken heart and a wicked sense of betrayal to grapple with. The only way she knew how to push through the pain she felt was to keep busy. Here in her store, among her staff and the beautiful clothes, shoes and accessories she'd carefully curated, she felt a measure of safety. The boutique served as a kind of physical buffer against her emotional turmoil.

Eliza ceased her pacing, coming to a stop behind the counter. Leaning her side against the edge, she exhaled. Even as she caught her breath, her eyes darted around the store. *Did I forget anything?*

Coretta walked up then. After studying Eliza's expression for a moment, she remarked, "If you're looking for something else to do, there's nothing left, boss lady."

She sighed. "It's that obvious, huh?"

Chuckling, Coretta nodded. "Yep. What I don't know is why you're wasting your weekend here in the first place. You know good and well that me and the staff can hold things down here while you get some rest."

"I know. Trust me, it's not a lack of faith in you that brought me here."

Coretta nodded. "I can tell. But I'm not going to press. It's not my place to get in your business. If you want to be here, it's not like I'm gonna try to send you home."

Eliza gave her a half smile. "I appreciate that."

"But I will tell you that you're out of luck on finding any more busy work, unless a customer comes in."

As Coretta turned to walk away, the bell over the door rang.

"Looks like you're in luck. I'll let you take this one, boss lady." Coretta winked as she disappeared into the stockroom.

Eliza turned toward the entrance and felt a shock wave of surprise go through her when she saw the familiar figure approaching the counter. "Jojo? What are you doing here?"

Jojo, clad in a Kendrick Lamar T-shirt, blue jeans and sneakers, wore a serious expression as she stopped on the other side of the counter. "Hi, Miss Eliza. I was hoping I could talk to you for a minute."

"Sure, I suppose." She stopped for a moment, studied Jojo. "Who brought you here?"

"My friend Maddie's mom. She and Maddie are waiting in the car outside."

Eliza felt her brow crease. "Do your parents know you're here?"

"No. But they know I'm with Maddie and her mom. Can we please talk? It won't take long, I promise."

Eliza didn't really know about all this, but the youngster seemed so earnest in her plea. "All right. Let's go sit down." She gestured to the over-stuffed ottomans set up near the fitting rooms. They walked over, taking seats on adjacent otto-mans. "So, what's this about, honey?"

"I know you're mad at my Dad. But could you please take him back?"

Surprised for the second time by this sweet young girl, Eliza tilted her head to one side. "That's why you came all the way over here?"

Jojo nodded. "I know it's probably not my place to get involved in this. But I felt like I had to at least try."

"I'm going to be honest with you, Jojo. I'm not really sure why you'd try to get us back together."

Jojo looked confused. "What do you mean?"

"Your dad told me about the sculpture at the

gallery, and why you vandalized it. If you were jealous of the time your dad spent working, then why are you okay with him spending so much time with me?"

"It's true, I didn't like that Dad was always working. And he did spend a lot of time with you. But with you, it's different."

"How so?" Eliza listened intently, eager to hear the answer.

"It's just that Dad was so happy when you were around. Now that you're mad at him, he's miserable. All he's done is sit on the pool deck, staring into the water. He's a mess."

Something tugged at Eliza's heart as she listened to Jojo describe her father's manner over the last couple of days. She could imagine him, silent and despondent, sitting by the pool just as his daughter described him. She could also see the concern in Jojo's eyes; it was obviously that concern that had brought her here to plead his case. She sighed. "I don't know, Jojo. Relationships can be complicated sometimes, in ways you don't understand just yet. It's not so simple as just taking him back."

With her brown eyes wide and hopeful, Jojo took a deep breath. "I get that. But if Dad was willing to give me a second chance after I messed up

Mr. Jace's sculpture, couldn't you at least try to give him a second chance, too?"

Try as she might, Eliza couldn't muster a good argument against Jojo's words. Maybe it was the logic behind what she'd said or the pleading look in the young girl's eyes. Maybe it was both. All Eliza knew was that she still loved Chris, and beyond that, she genuinely liked his bright, determined daughter.

Jojo gave her a small smile. "So, what do you say, Ms. Eliza?"

Eliza returned her smile. "I'll come over to see him tomorrow. How's that?"

Jojo's expression brightened, her smile widening to a grin. "Sounds great."

## Chapter 16

Late Sunday morning, Chris sat on the pool deck at his house, looking out over the mountains. The day was somewhat cool and hazy, which meant his view was obstructed by the fog hanging over the city. He didn't care, though. He hadn't come out on his deck to enjoy the view. It was his weekend with the kids, and he'd come out on the deck for the solitude.

Parts of him felt guilty about not spending time with the twins. Not that they seemed to mind. In the past, they'd loved playing board games with their dad, or spending time watching movies or television shows together. Now, as the twins embarked on their teenage years, they seemed more interested in their electronic devices and social media accounts than playing Scrabble with Dad. Their disinterest usually bothered him, but this weekend, it played right into his desire to be alone.

Still, he couldn't help being affected by Jojo's words about wanting more time with him. Raising teenagers confounded him most of the time, but he did his best to see to their needs without it costing him his sanity. Rather than overanalyze, he just tried to meet his children's' needs, even though they seemed to change moment to moment.

For now, though, Eliza consumed his mind. The three days since Eliza had kicked him out of her cottage, and out of her life, had been hellish. He'd gone through the days like a zombie, barely eating, spending his waking hours on the pool deck. Something about being near the water offered him a measure of comfort, though he didn't think anything would fully mend the ache in his chest.

He glanced to his right at the lounger that matched the one he reclined in. He could almost see her there, stretched out in nothing but his T-shirt. He closed his eyes against the memory, because he missed her so much, it physically hurt.

His traitorous mind took advantage of his eyes

being closed, and he imagined her atop him, as she had been the morning after they'd first made love. He could almost feel the weight of her body straddling his; the sweetness of her kiss. He could swear he felt her fingertips stroke his jawline. The sensation was so real, his eyes popped open.

He nearly fell off the lounger when he saw Eliza standing over him. He blinked a few times to see if she would disappear. But when she touched his cheek again, he knew she was real. Clasping his hand over hers, he spoke her name. "Eliza."

"Hi. Jack let me in." She offered a small smile. Her eyes raked over his body, encased in an old, faded T-shirt and blue sweatpants. "Wow. Jojo was right. You're looking pretty damn pitiful."

He knew she'd just dissed him, but he was so happy she'd come over, he didn't care. "Jojo?"

She nodded. "She came to the boutique last night. Told me you were miserable without me and asked me to please take you back. It was very endearing."

Chris decided then and there that his daughter could have whatever she wanted for Christmas. "I didn't send her."

"I know. She came on her own. She really loves you, Chris, and I have to say, I was touched by her concern for you."

*So am I.* He felt a smile tilt his lips, the first one he'd felt in days. "Listen, Eliza. I'm so glad you came. I just want to tell you again how sorry I am about…"

She placed her index finger over his lips, effectively silencing him. "You already apologized, and I forgive you."

"Because of Jojo?" He wished he could snatch the question back, but he had to know.

She shook her head. "No. Because I understand why you did what you did. You were right about Dad—he's got a lot of friends in high places. He probably could have carried out his threat to keep your career from getting off the ground."

He sighed, feeling relieved but still repentant. "Still. I should have stood up for you. For our love."

She tapped his leg. "Scoot over."

He folded his legs up, and she sat on the end of the lounger. "Do you remember what you said, about what us staying together back then might have meant for our career accomplishments?"

"Yeah, I remember."

"You were right about that, too." She gestured to their surroundings with her hands. "I mean, look at this place. You live on the side of a freaking mountain, and you're responsible for some of the most beautiful buildings around the country and the world. There's no way I would have wanted to stand in the way of you achieving all this."

He felt his heart turn over in his chest. He was so taken aback, he didn't know what to say.

"Don't you see, Chris? You're amazing. Your talent has taken you everywhere." She grabbed his hand. "In a way, it even led you back to me."

She was right, and her insight impressed him. He would never have been invited to join Prescott George if not for his success in architecture. His joining the organization and working his way up the ranks to become president of his chapter were what led him to be in the offices the day Eliza had walked back into his life.

He couldn't remember ever feeling so happy, not since the day the twins were born. "Does that mean you'll give me another chance?"

"Yes." She grinned, then leaned over for his kiss.

He wove his fingers into the silken weight of her hair, keeping her near while their tongues mated. An hour ago, he'd thought he'd lost her. Kissing her now felt like a gift, and he enjoyed every moment of the contact. When he finally released her, she looked a little dazed.

"I'm going to have to have it out with my parents, and I'm not looking forward to it." She sighed.

"I'll bet. Do you want me to go with you?"

"Nah. I'll handle it on my own." She ran a hand through her hair. "It's not going to be easy, but it's the adult thing to do. I guess it's like Dad always says. Life was better in the old days."

Hearing that phrase raised his brow. "Did you say, life was better in the old days?"

"Yeah. Dad says it all the time."

He narrowed his eyes. He'd seen that exact phrase in one of the newspaper articles reporting negatively about Prescott George. *Holy crap. Is the Colonel involved in this?*

She frowned, apparently noticing the change in his demeanor. "What's wrong, Chris?"

"It's just that one of the so-called anonymous sources that's spoken to the papers has used that phrase."

"Wow." Her eyes widened. "Until a few days ago, I never would have imagined my Dad to be so manipulative. But now, I don't know. I've definitely heard him and some of the old-timers grumbling about how things used to be at Prescott George."

"Well, I'm obviously going to have to look into this."

She waved him off. "I'll do it. Besides, I have to talk to him anyway. I'll let you know what I find out."

He nodded. If Eliza wanted to handle the situation with her father, he wouldn't stand in her way.

"I don't want to talk about this serious stuff anymore. That's not why I came over." Her expression changed then, and a wicked gleam came into her eyes. "So...how much longer are the twins going to be here?"

He smiled, knowing exactly why she'd asked that. Glancing at his gold wristwatch, he said, "Sheila will pick them up in the next couple of hours."

"Cool. I can wait." She winked, then got up from the lounger and started walking toward the door.

He watched the tempting sway of her hips, unable to take his eyes off her.

She stopped, looked at him. "Are you coming? There's no reason for you to stay out here moping anymore."

He heard the teasing in her tone, and he laughed. *She's really something else.* Climbing to his feet, he followed her inside the house.

Monday afternoon, Eliza left the boutique early and returned home. After she left her car at the cottage, she walked over to the main house. It was a good half mile, but she didn't mind. She needed the fresh air and the opportunity to clear her mind before what was sure to be a difficult conversation.

She entered the house by the side door, as she usually did, and stopped off in the kitchen to grab a soda. With the ice-cold can in hand, she went looking for her parents. She didn't have to search very long, because they were both sitting on the sofa in the den, watching television.

Natalie looked up when Eliza walked in. "Hey, honey. How are things at the store?"

She smiled, despite the ball of emotions rolling around inside her. "Things are great, Mom. Thanks for asking." She looked to her father. "Hi, Dad."

"Hey, pumpkin." He offered her an absent smile, not looking away from the TV.

That was as she'd expected. Since he'd retired from the navy, he spent a good amount of time on the couch, absorbed in his favorite shows. To her, it seemed as if he were trying to catch up on all the shows he'd missed during his years out at sea.

Crossing the space until she stood in front of the television, she announced, "Mom, Dad, I was hoping I could talk to you."

Vaughn Sr. leaned to his right, attempting to

scc around her. "Can it wait? I'm watching something."

She shook her head, because she knew better than to put the conversation off any longer than necessary. That would only lead to more anger and bitterness for her. "Sorry, Dad. I don't think it can wait."

Natalie, looking concerned, patted the sofa cushion next to her. "Come sit down, Eliza." Then she grabbed the remote from her husband's lap and flicked the TV off.

Eliza did as her mother asked, taking the seat between Natalie and the arm of the sofa.

From the other end of the sofa, Vaughn Sr. complained, "I was watching that."

"Hush up. Our baby girl has something important to say." Natalie put her arm around Eliza's shoulder. "Go ahead and say what's on your mind."

She drew a deep breath. "First of all, I've been seeing Chris Marland for quite a few weeks now."

Vaughn Sr. leaned forward in his seat, his face twisting with disapproval. "Oh, really."

"Yes." She briefly recounted running into him at Prescott George. "That's when this all got started. I didn't tell you we were seeing each other because I didn't think you'd be receptive, but that's not what I want to talk about."

Vaughn Sr. started on a rant. "Young lady, I don't know why you'd take up with Chris again, but I don't approve, and…"

"Excuse me, Dad. As I said, that's not what I want to talk about."

He frowned. "What, then?"

"I know you and Mom told Chris to break up with me when we dated before. Well, mostly you, Dad."

Natalie gasped. "Oh, goodness."

Eliza squeezed her mother's hand. "I'm guessing you didn't want any part in this, and that Dad pushed the issue."

Natalie hesitated for a moment, but finally nodded. "You know I believe in letting a man be head of the household, so I went along with what Vaughn Sr. wanted." Her words were laced with guilt. "I'm sorry, baby."

"It's okay, Mom." She gave her a kiss on the cheek. "I just want to get all this out in the open, but I'm not angry with you."

Vaughn Sr. sat stoic and silent. He stared straight ahead, but Eliza could see the tremble in his jaw.

Eliza spoke softly to him, careful to be respectful despite how she felt. "Dad, you know I love you. And I know you were trying to protect me.

But it wasn't fair for you to make a decision like this for me without even talking to me about it. I was young, but I was also an adult."

Vaughn Sr.'s frown relaxed into something more recalcitrant than angry. "You just don't understand what it's like to raise children, to worry every day about how their life will turn out. Will they be successful, happy, fulfilled? All I wanted was the very best for you, Eliza."

Natalie slipped from between them, and Eliza scooted over next to her father. "Dad, you raised us right and equipped us with everything we needed to live a good life. That included good judgment. You've taught me how to analyze a situation and make the right decisions. Can you just trust what you've taught me and let me make my own choices, please?"

He looked at her then, his eyes holding his apology. "I...I'll do my best. Forgive me, pumpkin. I was just trying to look out for you, but I see now that you can look out for yourself."

She smiled. "Thank you, Dad." She gave him a kiss on the forehead.

Natalie, standing by the coffee table, sniffled. "I'm getting out of here before you two have me crying."

"Too late, Mom," Eliza quipped as her mother fled the room and headed upstairs.

Left alone with her father, Eliza took the opportunity to bring up the other pressing issue on her mind. "Dad, can I ask you something?"

"No, I didn't run off any of your other boyfriends." He winked.

She laughed. "No, Dad, not that. It's about Prescott George. Do you know anything about the break-ins and all the other problems going on over there?"

Vaughn Sr. shook his head. "Nothing other than what I've read in the paper."

"So you weren't involved in any of it? Because I've heard you complaining about the new way things are done over there and how it dishonors tradition and all that."

He looked shocked, confused. "No, of course not. I'd never be involved in a crime."

"What about your friends? Do you think any of them would?"

He scratched his chin. "No. Jonathan Jace, Jordan's dad, is pretty annoyed about how the organization is run now, and so are a few of us other first-generation members. But no matter how much we disagree with what they're doing, we all have a special place in our heart for Prescott George.

It's a historic organization, and we wouldn't want to see it come to harm."

She nodded, seeing her father's sincerity. "Okay. I guess Chris and the chapter will have to keep digging to find out who's behind all this mess."

Vaughn Sr. leaned in close to her. "Actually, I've been doing some digging of my own. I've got plenty of free time on my hands since I retired, so I've been looking into it. You won't believe what I found out."

"What?"

"We think the culprits are members of Prescott George. Specifically, members of the Los Angeles chapter."

She stared, openmouthed. Realizing how she must look, she closed her mouth. Then she asked the obvious question. "Why would they do that?"

He shrugged. "Jealousy. It's a powerful motivator. And everything I've uncovered says that the Los Angeles chapter doesn't think the San Diego chapter should have won the Chapter of the Year award."

"Wow." She didn't know what to say to that. Prescott George was a prestigious organization, with high ideals, stringent membership requirements and an air of exclusivity in everything it did. She couldn't believe that cogent adults, let alone members of this storied organization, would stoop to such levels of pettiness. But as her father had said, jealousy could drive people to do things they wouldn't normally do.

"What's worse is I think the ringleader may be someone I know, someone I even considered a friend once." He shook his head. "It's a shame to have this kind of infighting going on in the organization. It's not what the founders stood for."

Eliza nodded. "Thanks for the intel, Dad. I see you've still got your reconnaissance skills."

He smiled. "Hey, once a sailor, always a sailor. Prescott George has meant a lot to me, and I'm not about to give up the ship."

Eliza pecked her day on the cheek. Her dad was still as corny as ever, but since he'd been such a big help, she'd let it slide.

## Chapter 17

Chris was in his living room Monday evening, reading an issue of *Architectural Digest*, when he heard his doorbell ring. Setting the magazine aside, he went to answer the door. When he opened it, he found Eliza standing there. Dressed in a long blue dress in a flowing fabric, she smiled.

"Hey. I've got some information for you about this Prescott George thing."

"Come on in." He stepped back to allow her inside. After they were seated comfortably on his sofa, he said, "I'm guessing you already talked to your dad."

She nodded. "Yes. I went over there earlier today. First, we dealt with the whole issue of him running you off back in the day."

"How'd he take that?"

"He wasn't happy about having me bring it up. I think he seemed a little embarrassed by what he did. Anyway, he apologized and agreed not to meddle in my life anymore, so I'd say we're square."

He blew out a breath. "Great. Hopefully he won't have any ill will toward me after this, either."

"I don't think so." She scooted closer to him. "Now, let me tell you what I found out about the Prescott George mystery."

He leaned in, listening intently while she relayed the details of her conversation with the Colonel. When she was finished, he shook his head in disbelief. "You mean to tell me that another chapter is responsible for all the turmoil around here? That this is an inside job?"

"Based on what Dad told me, yes. Recon was part of his navy work, and he's still got the old instincts. I really think he's onto something."

Taken aback by this new and unexpected revelation, Chris fell back against the sofa cushions. "Wow. Of all the things I thought you'd bring back to me, I never would have guessed this one."

"How do you feel after hearing all this?"

"Shocked and relieved. At least I have a lead now, and that will take the heat off Jojo."

Her brow crinkled. "What do you mean?"

"Well, since she admitted to vandalizing Jordan's sculpture, there's been a lot of chatter that she might also be behind some of our other problems. Now that we have this information, I think we can safely put those rumors to bed."

"That's good. But now that I've told you about the Los Angeles chapter, what are you going to do?" She studied his face, awaiting his answer.

"First, I've got to get in touch with the national office. They need to know about this, so they won't cancel our gala tomorrow night." He ran his hand over his forehead, then glanced at his watch. "This news came just in time. I've got an hour to contact them and stop them from canceling the party."

"Okay. I'll wait while you make the call."

He stepped into his office and put in a call to Dr. Clark. "Hello, Dr. Clark. I have some very important news regarding the issues with my chapter."

"Good," Dr. Clark said. "I'm eager to hear an explanation for the tomfoolery going on over there."

Chris spent the next few minutes explaining everything to the assistant director. "And all of this information is from Colonel Ellicott. He's been looking into things on our behalf."

"I see. Looks like the Colonel has better investigative skills than the private detective you all hired."

Chris chuckled. "I guess that's true. Anyway, I was hoping that considering this new information, you would reconsider canceling our gala tomorrow night."

"Of course. The gala will go on as scheduled. I'm actually grateful to hear this evidence, because we would have lost a lot of money on a last-minute cancellation."

Chris remembered bringing that up in their last conversation. "Good, then we're on the same page. If you don't mind my asking, sir, what action is the national organization going to take now?"

Dr. Clark sighed. "It pains me to have to do this, but we're going to have to put the Los Angeles chapter on probationary status. If they're behind this mess, it's indicative of a larger problem within their chapter, and that needs to be addressed before they can reclaim active status."

"Will there be arrests? Charges filed?"

"No, I don't think so. That's way more negative press than the national organization wants to deal with right now." Dr. Clark paused. "I think if we make the chapter confess their deeds to the national board, then take disciplinary action against the chapter, the guilty parties will see the error of their ways without getting law enforcement involved."

"That seems reasonable."

"Of course, I'll discuss this with the director and the board, but that's the best course of action in my opinion."

"Whatever the board thinks is best, the San Diego chapter will support it."

"That's very wise. Now, I've got to get busy on reining in the Los Angeles chapter. As for you, Mr. Marland, I believe you have a gala to prepare for." Dr. Clark disconnected the call.

A smiling Chris returned to the living room.

Eliza, still sitting on the sofa, turned his way when he walked in. "Anything you need me to do?"

"Yes. Go to the boutique and get your most beautiful gown."

She looked confused. "Why?"

"Because the gala is on, and I want you to be there on my arm."

Her only replay was a sultry smile that warmed his insides.

\* \* \*

As she walked arm in arm with Chris onto the deck of the *Star of India*, Eliza felt like a queen walking into her coronation. The tall ship, a national and state historic landmark, had circled the globe twenty-one times since its maiden voyage in 1863. Now the *Star of India*, along with a fleet of other historically significant ships, was docked in San Diego Bay to form the Maritime Museum of San Diego. As she took in the sights around her, she couldn't imagine a more unique venue for a party.

It was about an hour after sunset, but the ship was lit up as bright as day. Paper lanterns hung from the ship's moorings, illuminating the white-clothed tables and chairs set up around the deck. Near the bow, a buffet was set up, containing gastronomic delights of every kind. People dressed in their best formal wear milled around the space, engaged in conversation and enjoying the glasses of champagne being passed around by a troupe of tray-carrying waiters.

Chris looked very dapper in his coal black tuxedo, complete with silver vest and tie. She'd chosen to wear a white silk charmeuse cocktail dress. The one-shoulder design was sprinkled with clear crystals, and the hem grazed her midcalf. Anticipating the locale for tonight's event, she'd chosen a pair of metallic silver sandals with a kitten heel, as well as a matching wrap to shield her shoulders from the breeze flowing over San Diego Bay.

A waiter passed them as they moved toward a reserved table, and Chris took two glasses of champagne from his tray. Passing one to her, he smiled.

She accepted the glass and took a sip as they arrived at the table. Eliza stopped to give her brother Vaughn a quick hug. Vaughn, who'd come with his wife, Miranda, returned her embrace. If he was still miffed about his sister being involved with Chris, he didn't let it show. Perhaps Vaughn had taken time to consider how ridiculous it was for him to judge Eliza's relationship with Chris. After all, Vaughn and Miranda had barely known each other when they'd married, much to the disapproval of their parents. Things had turned out fine for them, and when Eliza looked at her brother and sister-in-law, she simply saw two people in love.

There were two other people at the table that Eliza didn't recognize, and after she and Chris were seated, he began the introductions. The man was famed sculptor Jordan Jace, and the attractive woman with him was his fiancée, Sasha Charles.

After they all exchanged greetings, the conversation around the table began flowing. They'd been talking for a few moments when Jojo walked up. She looked very pretty in her peach A-line dress. Behind her stood her twin brother, Jack, who looked less than happy about having to wear a tuxedo.

The kids both greeted everyone at the table, and Jojo leaned over to hug Eliza's shoulders. Eliza, both surprised and touched, returned the gesture. Jojo then moved to Chris's side, whispering something in his ear before she and Jack faded back into the crowd of partygoers.

"What was that about?" Eliza asked.

Chris waved her off. "Nothing much." He turned his attention to Jordan. "So, Jordan, how has Jojo been doing at the studio?"

"Great. She's been very helpful and cooperative."

"I'm glad to hear it. And again, I really appreciate you letting her work with you to make up for what she did." Chris reached out to shake his friend's hand.

"No problem." Jordan offered a smile.

The group broke up for a while as they danced to the music being played over the loudspeakers. The tunes, ranging from up-tempo jazz to classic R&B, kept the party going, and Eliza enjoyed twirling around the dance floor. When the slow jams played, she relished the feeling of their bodies pressed close together as they swayed to the rhythm.

Within an hour or so, the six of them were back at the table, nibbling on plates of food from the buffet. For a while, the only sound at the table was the clinking of utensils against the china plates.

Miranda spoke up, restarting the conversation. "So, I don't think I've told you all, but I'm planning to open a luxury bed-and-breakfast in Malibu. Vaughn and I are renewing our vows next week, and it's been kind of crazy planning that and the B and B at the same time, but we'll manage."

"Wow, you've got a lot going on." Sasha took a sip from her champagne flute. "Jordan and I are getting married next fall, so I know how much work goes into wedding planning."

"Yeah. We're going to keep things simple, though. You two should definitely honeymoon at my place," Miranda offered. "It will be open and in full swing by then."

"What do you think?" Sasha squeezed Jordan's hand.

"Whatever you want, baby." He gave her a peck on the lips.

Eliza smiled, leaning closer to Chris. He turned

and kissed her, then winked. That started her giggling, and she covered her mouth with her hand.

Vaughn shook his head. "Look at you two. You're acting just like you did back in the day."

"Look at them, Vaughn." Miranda gestured toward them. "With him in that black tuxedo and her in the white dress, they look just like the figurines on top of a wedding cake."

"Funny you should mention that," Chris said as he slid his chair back from the table and stood. "I have something to say."

A confused Eliza watched as Jack and Jojo reappeared on opposite sides of their father. Only this time, they weren't empty-handed. Jojo handed Eliza a bouquet of two dozen long-stemmed pink roses. She took the flowers, cradling them in her arms as she tried to figure out what was going on.

She saw Jack smile, a rare occurrence indeed, as he passed his father a small black velvet box. Before she could make the connection, Chris dropped to his knee.

Eliza clasped a hand over her mouth.

The music that had been playing over the loudspeakers was turned down, and he spoke in a booming voice.

"Eliza Ellicott, I was foolish enough to leave you behind once, but I'll never be that foolish again." He opened the box, revealing a large princess-cut diamond ring on a rose-gold band. "Will you be my wife? Jojo, Jack and I would be honored to have you as part of our family."

Tears sprang to her eyes, and she nodded vigorously, unable to speak around the ball of emotion in her throat. He slid the ring onto her finger, and they both stood. As he drew her into his arms, she turned her face up to his kiss while thunderous applause sounded around them.

The program went on as scheduled, and Eliza watched with pride as Chris accepted the national award on behalf of his chapter. More dancing followed the ceremony, then drinking and celebrating. As the midnight hour drew near, Chris sent Jojo and Jack home with his driver.

As they walked down the gangplank and onto the dock holding hands, Eliza looked up at Chris. "So, what are we doing tonight?"

"I thought we'd have a proper celebration of our engagement."

She smiled. "Sounds fantastic, but where are we going? My feet are killing me from all that dancing."

"Don't worry, we're not going far." He led her down the dock until they stopped in front of a small yacht that was anchored a few slips away from the *Star of India*. "This is my boat."

She read the name off the bow. "The SS *Babydoll*?" Tears sprang to her eyes for the second time that night. "That's the nickname you used to call me by."

"Yep." He pulled her to him, gave her a kiss on the forehead. "I bought it to celebrate my first European design about six years ago."

"Christopher Marland, you charmer, you."

"If you think I'm so great now, wait until I get you below deck. I'm going to make love to you until they can hear you screaming my name on the other side of the bay." He kissed her again, this time on the lips. "I love you, Eliza."

"I love you, too, Chris."

Before she could say anything else, he swept her up into his arms as if she weighed nothing. Draping her arms around his neck, she hung on as he carried her onboard the ship.

\* \* \* \* \*

KIMANI ROMANCE

# COMING NEXT MONTH
## Available May 22, 2018

## #573 WHEN I'M WITH YOU
### *The Lawsons of Louisiana* • by Donna Hill
Longtime New Orleans bachelor Rafe Lawson is ready to tie the knot.
His heart has been captured by the gorgeous Avery Richards. Then the media
descends, jeopardizing her Secret Service career—and their imminent wedding.
But it's the unexpected return of Rafe's first love that could cost the tycoon
everything.

## #574 PLEASURE IN HIS KISS
### *Love in the Hamptons* • by Pamela Yaye
Beauty blogger and owner of the Hamptons's hottest salon Karma Sullivan
has been swept off her feet by judge Morrison Drake. But she knows their
passion-filled nights must end. She can't let her family secret derail Morrison's
ambitious career plan. Even if it means giving up the man she loves...

## #575 TEMPTING THE BEAUTY QUEEN
### *Once Upon a Tiara* • by Carolyn Hector
If Kenzie Swayne didn't require a date for a string
of upcoming weddings, she'd turn Ramon Torres's
offer down flat. The gorgeous entrepreneur stood
her up once already. Now Ramon needs Kenzie's
expertise for a new business venture. But when
past secrets are revealed, can Ramon make Kenzie
his—forever?

## #576 WHEREVER YOU ARE
### *The Jacksons of Ann Arbor* • by Elle Wright
Avery Montgomery created a hit show about her
old neighborhood, but she can't reveal the real
reason she left town. Dr. Elwood Jackson has never
forgiven Avery for leaving. But when a crisis lands
her in El's emergency room, passion sparks hotter
than before. Will this be their second chance?

# Get 2 Free Books,
## Plus 2 Free Gifts—
### just for trying the
### Reader Service!

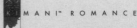

They were a natural fit with each other, as if living under
the same roof was something they'd always done. Rafe
was attentive, but gave her space. He possessed chef-like
skills in the kitchen, a penchant for neatness—she never
had to step over discarded clothing or clean up after a
meal—and above all he was a master in the bedroom and
made her see heaven on a regular basis. This man was
going to be her husband. Sometimes, when she looked
at him or held him tight between her thighs, she couldn't
believe that Rafe Lawson was hers. What she wanted was
just the two of them, but marrying Rafe was marrying
his large, controlling family.

"You sure you'll be okay until I get back from N'awlins?" He wiped off the countertop with a damp cloth.

She shimmied onto the bar stool at the island counter and extended her hands to Rafe. He took two long steps and was in front of her. He raised her hands to his lips and kissed the insides of her palms.

"I'll be fine, and right here when you get back." She leaned in to kiss him.

"Hmm, I can change my plans," he said against her lips, "and stay here, which is what I'd rather do." He caressed her hips.

Avery giggled. "Me, too, but you've been gone long enough. Take care of your business."

He stepped deep between her legs. "Business can wait." He threaded his fingers through the hair at the nape of her neck, dipped his head and kissed her collarbone.

Avery sucked in a breath of desire and instinctively tightened her legs around him. "You're going to be late," she whispered.

He brushed his lips along her neck, nibbled the lobe of her ear. "Privilege is the perk of owning your own plane. Can't leave without me."

*Don't miss WHEN I'M WITH YOU*
*by Donna Hill, available June 2018*
*wherever Harlequin® Kimani Romance™ books*
*and ebooks are sold.*